"Amusing . . . playful . . . delightfully postmodern . . . a cinematic work of fiction. . . . Part Beckett, part Woody Allen."

—*Kirkus Reviews*

"An utterly enchanting book about the New York that all of us know. These fables are crammed with the daydreams and nightmares which are normal for every native, and we can rejoice that Mark Ciabattari has been at large in our city—and that he understands us so well."

—NORA SAYRE, AUTHOR OF
Running Time

"Immensely entertaining . . . a wonderfully amusing collection of fantastic tales—all clever and inventive."

—THOMAS BENDER, AUTHOR OF
New York Intellect

D0557864

Mark Ciabattari is a New Yorker who writes fiction and has taught at NYU, Yeshiva University, and Baruch/CUNY.

Istvan Banyai is a Hungarian-born illustrator whose work is well known in both Europe and America. He lives in Los Angeles.

Ωbelisk

DREAMS OF
AN IMAGINARY
NEW YORKER
NAMED RIZZOLI

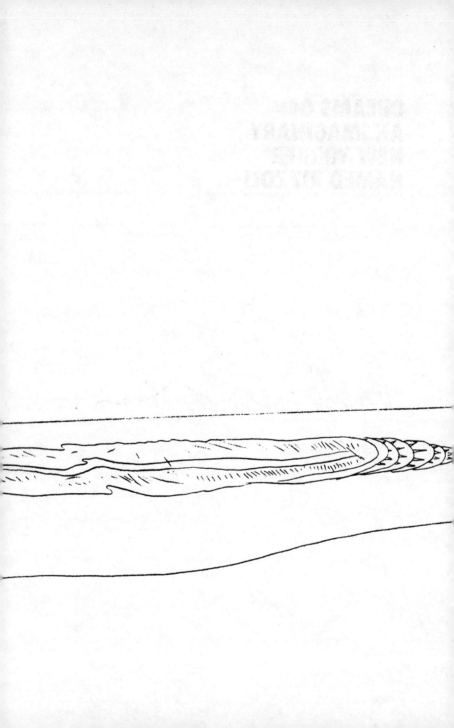

DREAMS OF
AN IMAGINARY
NEW YORKER
NAMED RIZZOLI

Mark Ciabattari

ILLUSTRATED BY ISTVAN BANYAI

A Dutton Obelisk Paperback
E. P. DUTTON / NEW YORK

Published in the United States by Obelisk Books, E. P. Dutton,
a division of Penguin Books USA Inc.,
2 Park Avenue, New York, N.Y. 10016.

Published simultaneously in Canada by
Fitzhenry and Whiteside,
Limited, Toronto.

Library of Congress Cataloging-in-Publication Data

Ciabattari, Mark.
  Dreams of an imaginary New Yorker named Rizzoli / Mark
Ciabattari; illustrated by Istvan Banyai. — 1st ed.
      p. cm.
  ISBN 0-525-48539-2
  I. Title.
PS3553.I29D74   1990
813'.54—dc20   89-34978
                                                  CIP

Book package by Square Moon Productions
Designer: Diane Goldsmith
Editor: Jane Zimmerman

10 9 8 7 6 5 4 3 2 1

First Edition

CONTENTS

To Jane, for all the years of love and encouragement,
and to Scott, for the future

A RECURRING DREAM OF RIZZOLI WATCHING HIS FAVORITE TV PERSONALITY   Every night Rizzoli goes home to his own special TV set. It plays back to him scenes from his past in living color: a scene from that day maybe, or one earlier in his life. The set has two channels.

Tonight, as usual, he selects Channel One, the channel that gives him the greatest pleasure. The picture comes in: Immediately Rizzoli sees himself there on the TV screen as he was two weeks ago, asking his boss for a raise.

"I'm so poised," he thinks. He has seen himself in this scene on Channel One many times in the past two weeks. "Now, Mr. Whittaker," he is saying to his boss, "I have, after all, grown up with this concern. . ." As he pauses before continuing, Rizzoli finishes the sentence for himself even before he says it on the screen, knowing all his good lines by heart: " . . . so possibly you ought to consider my value at this time to another company. I am not speaking of a competitor—not necessarily."

"I had Whittaker right where I wanted him," Rizzoli comments aloud, just as the TV screen goes all fuzzy.

"SON-OF-A-BITCH!" Rizzoli screams. There is something wrong with his set. Every now and then it does this. "No, no. Not this!"

The picture comes back on. "Oh, no," Rizzoli mutters. It's Channel Two, the one he *doesn't* want to watch. There he is in the same scene saying, ". . . so possibly you ought to consider my value. . ." Now the tip of his white shirt is hanging out of his fly, which is half open.

Rizzoli curses the TV and swears he is going to get a

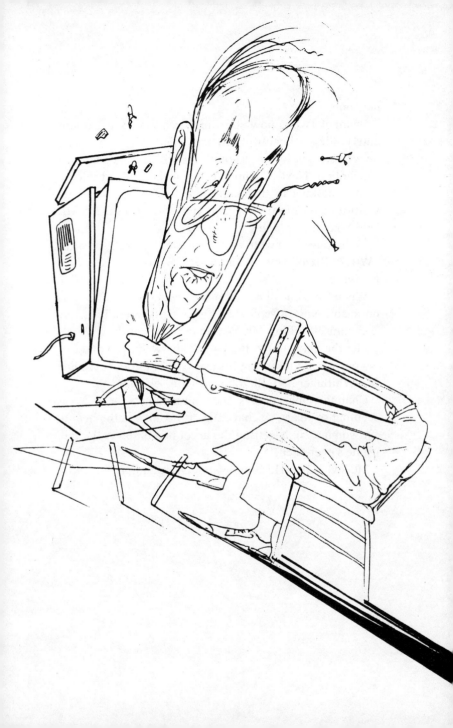

new one.

Channel Two is now showing Rizzoli in an apartment entertaining a beautiful woman client whose business he wants to get for his account. He will see her soon at a convention. Next, Channel Two shows him at the convention talking to this same beautiful woman and revealing a company secret that he promised Mr. Whittaker never to tell.

"Why does it have to do this to me?" Rizzoli screams. "WHY?" Rizzoli gets up and leaves the room. *I hate Two*, he thinks.

When he comes back into the room, Channel One is on again. Now Rizzoli sees himself as he really is. He sees himself telling Mr. Whittaker confidently, "What's under the hat is under the hat. It's between you and me. No one else." Observing his own self-confidence, seeing Mr. Whittaker nod, Rizzoli trusts himself again.

Channel One replays the convention. There he is seeming so suave, so charming, as he talks to the beautiful woman. He is getting the account. Rizzoli is the tallest he's ever been.

He loves One. He could watch One all night.

THE DREAM OF Rizzoli dreams that he is headed for
THE REASONABLE MAN an appointment with his
WHO LOVES CATS analyst who has an office in a
brownstone on 75th between Columbus and Amsterdam. Coming from Central Park, Rizzoli walks west
along 75th Street.

He has his head down, preoccupied with the dream
he wants to discuss with Dr. Toltaroff. He doesn't notice
the strange pair until they are almost alongside him. Just
as they pass, he catches a glimpse of them. He turns and
stares. He can't believe it. *It's like the dream!*

A big dog with his head up to Rizzoli's shoulder is
walking a small human whose head barely comes to
Rizzoli's knee. The person is on a leash, which the dog
holds in its mouth. The human is armed with a semi-
automatic rifle strapped across the shoulder and a bullet
belt around the waist. What is really strange, though, is
that from the back, the woman looks exactly like
Rizzoli's landlady, Mrs. Lundy.

At the corner, the two old guys who sell plants and
pots are standing and talking. Rizzoli asks, "Did you see
that?"

"Yeah! That mutt walking Mrs. Lundy. That's nothing," the one guys says. "For chrissake, take a look
around you. You ever seen anything like this? Take a
look!"

"Mother of God," Rizzoli says, turning to look down
Columbus. "Jumpin' Jesus!" Everywhere he looks there
are huge dogs out walking little armed humans. He and
the guys on the corner are the only humans Rizzoli can
see who are normal sized.

Rizzoli rushes across Columbus and along 75th to his

analyst's. This street is less crowded. Still, here and there, Rizzoli sees dogs walking armed humans.

He hurries to his analyst's front door and rings the bell. As he waits to be buzzed in, Rizzoli stands at the top of the stoop and watches a bulldog walk a little businessman by. Just as he passes the bottom of the steps, the little businessman trains his rifle on Rizzoli. "BANG! BANG!" the little businessman hollers. Rizzoli jumps. The little fellow laughs as the bulldog pulls the leash to jerk the little businessman along.

Down the block there are two little humans who are loose, dragging their leashes and shooting at one another. The little businessman fires a couple of rounds in their direction, before the bulldog drags him past.

Finally, the buzzer lets Rizzoli in. He scurries down the hallway to the waiting room of Dr. Toltaroff's office. While in the waiting room, Rizzoli worries about what he will do if Dr. Toltaroff comes out pint sized and led by a big dog. When Dr. Toltaroff opens the door and invites Rizzoli in for his hour, Rizzoli is greatly relieved to see that his doctor is normal sized.

Nothing to worry about, guy, he tells himself—his mind was only playing a little trick on him out there in the street.

Rizzoli lies down on the couch. He decides right off not to mention anything about what he thought he saw coming over here. *First, I'll get his reaction to the dream*, Rizzoli thinks. *Then maybe I'll bring up the other*.

"I had a dream last night," Rizzoli says.

"Do you want to tell me about it?" the doctor asks.

"In this dream," Rizzoli says, "I was a stray human in a world where dogs three times larger had little people for pets. They walked the little humans around the streets on leashes, like humans walk dogs in real life?" Rizzoli listens carefully to find out whether Dr. Toltaroff agrees that in "real life" people still walk dogs, not the other way around. He doesn't correct Rizzoli, so Rizzoli goes on.

"The people were all armed," Rizzoli says, "and on leashes that the dogs held in their teeth. Know how real dogs on leashes sometimes growl at one another when they pass?"

"Yes."

"Same thing in the dream, only the humans on leashes would fire off a few rounds into the air as they went by." Dr. Toltaroff is silent. "The dogs were kind, quite kind, really. But these humans were vicious. If they broke loose from their leashes they would have a fight, shooting to wound or kill. If the dogs didn't pull them apart, they'd kill each other."

"Did this frighten you?" Dr. Toltaroff asks.

"No," Rizzoli explains. "Because in the dream I was an outlaw human, feared by the other humans and the dogs alike. In this dream there were signs everywhere saying 'All Humans Must Be Leashed,' but I was not on any leash. I had no dog as a master. NO DOG!" Rizzoli gets more and more excited as he recalls the dangers of his dream. "I was hunted!"

"Why?" Dr. Toltaroff.

"No dog," Rizzoli repeats. "So I was hunted and I had no choice."

"No choice?"

"But to try to defend myself."

"You were armed?"

"You bet," Rizzoli says. "They came up on me in Central Park, all these human-catchers, people who do the dirty work for the dogs. The dogs themselves were kind, remember?"

"I remember."

"Not the humans. They were vicious—always on the lookout for strays, fugitives from dog justice. A band of these human-catchers found me holed up in the castle in Central Park. I was the biggest outlaw human around. They surrounded the castle. They wanted me dead or alive. They were going to put me before the firing squad anyway, so I had no choice. I killed twenty, maybe twenty-five of the little guys before they stormed the place, and more of them as they came. BANG! BANG! RAT-A-TAT! BANG! BANG! RAT-A-TAT! They all had semiautomatics, and so did I. I took out five of them at a clip, RAT-A-TAT!"

Rizzoli stops talking abruptly.

After a long silence Dr. Toltaroff asks, "Is that all?"

"They shot me," Rizzoli says. "You know how that is, same old thing: I woke up before I died. You can never die in your dreams."

"Really?" the doctor asks.

What does he mean by THAT? JEEZUS...! "You mean you *can* croak in your dreams?"

Dr. Toltaroff says nothing.

Rizzoli looks at his watch. There are five minutes left. He stares at the ceiling, trying to remember if there is anything else about the dream he ought to tell the doctor. When Dr. Toltaroff says it's time, Rizzoli sits up. He sees the doctor is coming around from behind his desk. He has turned into a giant black Labrador retriever.

Rizzoli looks down at himself. He has shrunk. His feet are now a long way from the end of the couch, and—as he looks down—he sees it is a long way to the floor. He carefully slides over the edge while hugging the couch cushion until his feet touch the floor.

Dr. Toltaroff the dog fastens a collar around little Rizzoli's neck.

"Are you taking me out for a walk, doctor?" little Rizzoli asks.

The doctor dog looks at him with a blank expression.

Can't the mutt talk? little Rizzoli wonders.

The dog takes little Rizzoli's leash in his mouth and starts for the door. *We are going outside*, Rizzoli concludes. *But he's forgetting I'm not armed.*

"Doctor, to go outside, I need a gun."

The dog gives him the same blank look.

"I NEED A GUN!" little Rizzoli yells.

Nothing.

Rizzoli digs in his heels, screaming, "I need a gun to go out there with all those vicious little humans!"

Dr. Toltaroff the dog jerks little Rizzoli out the door by his leash.

Dingaling mutt is taking me out without a gun!

At the front door, little Rizzoli again tries to stay put, but the doctor dog yanks him out and down the steps.

On the sidewalk, the first little human that little Rizzoli sees moves toward him, firing in the air all the while. Another rushes across the street towards little Rizzoli, pulling his dog behind him.

Dr. Toltaroff the dog lets go of little Rizzoli's leash. Little Rizzoli panics and scurries out into the street where he is suddenly surrounded. Little armed humans are closing in on him from all sides. One is little Mrs. Lundy. She stares at him, steely eyed, shooting into the air as she comes nearer. *Not Mrs. Lundy. Doesn't she see that it's me?* In desperation, Rizzoli lies down on his back in the middle of the street.

The little armed humans look at him lying there, belly-up, unarmed. They sniff at him. They lower their guns and walk away.

But when the little truck driver accidentally bumps into Mrs. Lundy, these two start shooting it out. Rizzoli rolls under a car and lies there while the dogs come and break it up. Rizzoli feels relieved.

All in all, he thinks still lying under the car, *I don't feel so bad now that I know going belly-up works.*

When all is quiet, Rizzoli scurries over to where Dr. Toltaroff is standing. The dog reaches down and undoes Rizzoli's leash.

Rizzoli can sense the danger in being free and un-armed. *What the hell. I'll give it a try,* he thinks. *Can't hurt.*

RIZZOLI DREAMS OF BEING LOST IN THE LAND OF THE CUD FOLK Rizzoli dreams he is sitting in a chair in the living room of a family of strangers. There is an awkward silence. Rizzoli doesn't know how to begin.

Rizzoli notices various framed messages hanging up on the walls:

Good Talk Is Like a Hiccup. It Comes Back Up Again.
The Everyday Repeats the Best in Conversation.

Rizzoli sees a longer message on the far wall:

The first time you hear what is said.
The second time you decide if you want to know what is said.
The third time you decide if you want to analyze what is said.

It goes on and on. "The fourth time. . . . The fifth time. . . ."

"Just before you arrived," the husband says to Rizzoli, "I went out to the kitchen, to the refrigerator. I opened it and took out bread, bologna, prosciutto, lettuce, tomatoes, cheddar cheese—the mild variety—and pickles."

He pauses. Rizzoli smiles politely.

"I made a sandwich of that," the man continues. "Then I looked for the mayonnaise and mustard. I looked everywhere. We were out. I had to eat my sandwich dry. I hate that."

"I know what you mean," Rizzoli says. He starts to say something, but the man interrupts him.

"Just before you arrived," the man begins again, "I

went out to the kitchen, to the refrigerator. I opened it . . ." He tells the whole story a second time, verbatim. Then he begins a third time, verbatim. He finishes and tells the same story a fourth time, verbatim.

Rizzoli keeps smiling. He asks questions, but the man ignores them.

After he tells the story the fifth time, the man stops and asks, "What about you, Rizzoli?"

Rizzoli's turn. He tells a story about making a sandwich in the middle of the night once and mistaking a bowl of whipped cream for mayonnaise because he didn't have his glasses on. He is supposed to repeat the story, he realizes, but he doesn't really remember it. *Anyway*, he thinks, *the guy isn't listening.*

Rizzoli tells another story, but the man isn't listening. Now it seems to be the wife's turn. "An hour ago, you know what I did, Rizzoli? My husband told you what he did, but do you know what I did?"

"What?"

"I got up from this chair, walked into that bedroom, and straightened the bed. I smoothed the wrinkles out of the red, blue, and green comforter. Then you know what I did?"

"What?" Rizzoli asks.

"I got up from this chair, walked into that bedroom, and straightened the bed. I smoothed the wrinkles out of the red, blue, and green comforter. Then you know what I did?"

"No," Rizzoli says.

"I came back in here when the phone rang. It was a wrong number, so I hung up. Then I filled this pitcher and went around watering the plants. First the Boston fern there, then the Swedish ivy here . . ." She goes on telling her long story in great detail.

Rizzoli tries to be polite and ask questions, but she goes right on as if she were reciting. The story ends; it has no point.

She pauses, then begins, "An hour ago, you know what I did, Rizzoli? My husband told you what he did, but do you know what I did?"

"What?" Rizzoli asks, thinking, *Where am I?*

"I got up from this chair, walked into that bedroom . . ."

Staten Island?

". . . the wrinkles . . ."

Jersey?

". . . filled this pitcher . . ."

Far Far Rockaway?

RIZZOLI DREAMS Rizzoli looks at himself in the
OF THE GREAT mirror first thing in the morning and
GRAFFITI CATASTROPHE sees graffiti all over his
forehead, cheeks, chin, and throat. It looks like Japanese
lettering done by red, green, and black marker pens,
and overwritten with a scribble. In the corner near his
eye is the signature "G-MAN," the only word legible to
Rizzoli. "Bastard got in last night and did me in my
sleep again!" Rizzoli shouts.

Rizzoli quickly throws on his clothes and dashes out
the door. On the next floor down from his apartment, he
sees a sad sight. Mrs. Lundy stands in front of her door;
she has graffiti all over her face, arms, even her thick
stockings. "Rizzoli, he got you too?"

"We're going to put a stop to this," Rizzoli tells her.
"Once and for all." They go down the stairs and out into
the street.

The NYPD policemen lining the block see them. One
shouts, "No, No!" Another turns to his partner and asks,
"How did the graffiti bandit get through again?" Another implores, "How come we can't stop him?"

"You tell me," Rizzoli says. They hang their heads.

"Come on. Quit the sniveling. I want more alligators
in that moat," Rizzoli says. He looks at the deep trench
that circles his block and at the snarling alligators swim-
ming there. He can't believe this graffiti guy ever got
over the moat and through the cordon, but somehow he
did.

The other neighbors are all out on the street, complaining. They, too, have graffiti painted over them.
*Graffiti man got the whole block again . . . The second time
in a week, dammit,* Rizzoli thinks.

He looks up and sees the police staring down from the rooftops, shaking their heads in disbelief.

"Mother of God," one cop says, looking heavenward. "Help us, please."

Soon the Mayor arrives on the scene. "We New Yorkers support the great, great people on this magnificent block now under terrible siege . . ."

The people interrupt him, shouting, "MORE POLICE! MORE ALLIGATORS!" They have heard the Mayor give this speech before. They want to pin him down.

"We New Yorkers will not stand to have the people on this block painted with graffiti . . ."

"MORE POLICE!"

". . . and we will do whatever is necessary . . ."

"MORE ALLIGATORS!"

The Mayor has come prepared; he has more police and alligators on the way. Even as he speaks, the alligators are dumped in the moat and new troops take their posts, linking arms with those who were there before.

"And I have a new strategy," the Mayor announces. He has the policemen line up Rizzoli and the others in the crowd. One policeman moves along, painting them all with whitewash from head to toe. "There. You're clean again," says the Mayor. To the gathered press the Mayor says, "Write this: 'We dare the graffiti criminal to deface any one of these clean, decent New Yorkers.' "

The next morning, Rizzoli wakes up and looks in the mirror. Nothing.

Rizzoli wakes up the second morning and looks in the mirror. He is still all white.

The third morning Rizzoli gets up and looks in the mirror and sees "XXXXXXXX" written on his

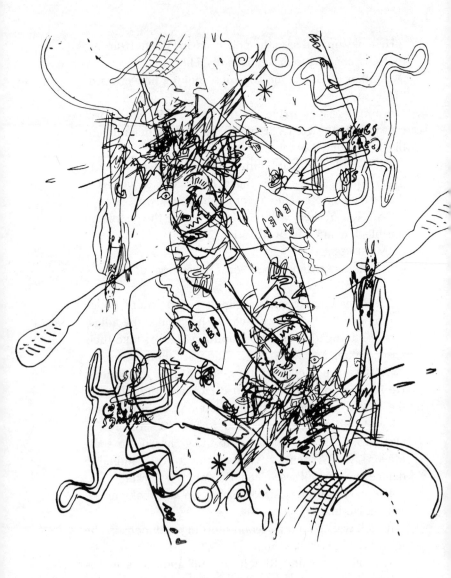

forehead in a black marker.

In fifteen minutes Rizzoli and his defaced neighbors are once again convened in the street. They are angry.

"I am giving up," the Mayor tells them. "I cannot justify using thirty-eight percent of the force to protect just one block in this huge city. This will pass. You have to wait, that's all."

The crowd boos.

"Quiet down!" the Mayor shouts. "I have ordered all the police back to their beats. Crime is on the rampage elsewhere in this great, great city."

More boos.

"The moat will be filled in," the Mayor continues, "and the streets surrouding this block returned to normal."

As the crowd steadily boos, the Mayor leaves.

The next morning, Rizzoli wakes up and throws off the covers. *No. No!* He looks like the tattooed man who he remembers seeing at a carnival when he was little. *G-Man got me in the night, all right.*

Rizzoli goes into the living room and turns on the TV to see if the local stations have anything about the graffiti guy. They do: a panel discussion.

"The lower classes used to be invisible. They won't stand for that anymore. They want the middle class to know they are down there," a prominent New York novelist is saying. "That's why they paint graffiti on the people who live on this middle-income block. They are saying, 'Yoo-hoo, we're here. You can't ignore us!' "

"Shut up, BREAD BRAIN!" Rizzoli screams.

A German journalist who critiques American culture gives his view: ". . . When Americans of the all-important middle class are victimized at random—if you will—then your American Dream ist kaput." He points at a blow-up of a New Yorker in an expensive business suit holding a custom leather attaché case. The businessman's face, neck, and hands are covered with purple and red graffiti. "Would you aspire to be this hapless fellow?"

A panel participant who has been masked all this time, speaks up: "We own the night!" He begins to spraypaint the German journalist, the novelist, the commentator, and the other panel participants. He paints the furniture on the set, the microphones, and finishes by spraying the lens of the camera with his signature: G-MAN.

"That's the son-of-a-bitch who got me!" Rizzoli yells. "TAKE THAT MASK OFF, LILY LIVER!"

The German and the novelist, speaking intensely through their markings, begin to discuss possible remedies with the commentator. It is clear that they know of none, calling this a fad that will just have to pass.

Rizzoli knows they're right. He'll have to wait, however long it will take.

In conclusion, the art dealer on the panel, himself brightly painted, advises the viewers not to try to wash the graffiti off: "It would help if you could learn to appreciate what it is that is scrawled all over you. It is art. You are art. Treasure that." He ends by advising people to have themselves shellacked so that the piece of art they are is rendered permanent. "That way, in your will, you can bequeath your skin as original artwork."

RIZZOLI DREAMS Rizzoli dreams of sitting in his of-
OF DRASTIC CHANGES fice when Eldridge, the
AT THE OFFICE mailroom boy, comes in.

"Just put them on the desk there," Rizzoli says, gestur-
ing toward the papers in Eldridge's hand. Rizzoli is busy
with a report.

"You got to move out," says Eldridge, "I'm in your
office now."

"Just put those there," Rizzoli repeats, not looking up.

"I'm serious."

"Sure you are, Eldridge." Rizzoli looks up, laughing.

"This company has been reorganized," Eldridge says.

"Sure it has, Eldridge." Rizzoli is impatient. *Fucking
Eldridge has never played with a full deck*, he thinks, but
Rizzoli knows from experience that there is only one
way to get rid of him—humor him. "Okay, Eldridge, I'll
play along. Who says this company is being
reorganized?"

"Guy in Chicago says."

"Who's that?" Rizzoli is impatient but is still trying to
be polite. He swears once again to see to it himself that
Eldridge is fired.

"Peter MacArthur III, Chairman of the Board, Axis
International, Inc." Eldridge reads from a memo.

MacArthur is the Chairman, Rizzoli knows, but little
or nothing else is known about him. No one in the company has ever seen him.

"This memo is dated a week ago," Eldridge says and
continues reading: "To President David C. Whittaker
(that's the one down in the mailroom today), Miles Company, Food Branch: Nutrient, Health, Recreation, and
Cosmetics Division of Axis International, Inc., Chicago,

Illinois, 55701." Eldridge goes on:

Dear President Whittaker,

As of February 12 *("That's today"),* I want you to reorganize your staff on the basis of physical power—brute strength, if you will. Whoever is the strongest individual in your company, I want that man (or woman) made President; the second strongest, the General Manager; the third strongest, the Head of Sales, etcetera, etcetera. If there is any question as to who may qualify for a certain position, I recommend first arm wrestling, then a weight lifting contest and, as the best option of all, a prize fight (to be held in your company gymnasium) until the best man (or woman) wins. Since we are an equal opportunity employer, after the new staff is in place, any employee has the right to fight another for any job at any time.

My reason for doing this is our industry is getting highly competitive, and we need the most aggressive, intimidating leadership possible if Miles Company is to win a greater share of the market so that Axis will continue to be the industry leader.

Let there be no misunderstanding. It is not that Axis is down-grading knowledge and experience. It is simply that we are putting them in the service of force. Management experts agree that for the future market, knowledge will be no match for force. The future is now, so Axis must prepare.

In conclusion, I will trust you will carry this out promptly and I am sorry, David, for your instant demotion. It is nothing personal. In your instance, age is clearly the culprit. We do appreciate your many years of service with Axis International, Inc.

(Signed) Peter MacArthur III

Chairman of the Board of Axis International, Inc.
Chicago, Illinois.

P.S. My orders are for the new President to have his new staff on a rigorous jogging and weight program, even more extensive than we have now. Have it be mandatory for all. Also, open invitational boxing matches—suggest smokers every two weeks.

P.S.S. New corporate neckties are mandatory. Dark blue with red, small-print "Kick Ass" all over them.

Eldridge hands the memo to Rizzoli. It is accurate. Rizzoli reads an attached letter from President Whittaker agreeing to the demotion, finding the letter "naturally unsettling but necessary for a strong Axis future." It is President Whittaker's familiar signature.

"So I'm third-in-charge," Eldridge says, "because I can kick everybody's ass in this company except for two guys I think can take me—the new Company President and his second-in-charge, that's John Schiavone, the trucker, and the warehouseman, Phil Kushernik.

"You, Rizzoli, ought to try for the mailroom. You can head it up. You ought to be able to kick shit out of the old president. The only one who might give you some trouble is Shadely."

SHADELY? "Not Shadely," Rizzoli blurts, incredulous that he again will be pitted with his nemesis for . . . *a slot in the MAIL ROOM??*

In a flash, his whole five-year-long rivalry with Shadely passes through Rizzoli's mind, beginning when Mr. Whittaker hired Rizzoli over Shadely and then, two months later, hired Shadely, too, after all. *Shmuck Shadely's always resented being second best to me in Mr. Whittaker's mind and Whittaker giving me this promotion last month really set Shadely off. That snake Shadely.* This is the worst news of all for Rizzoli, even worse than Eldridge taking his job. *Shadely.* His stomach is in knots already.

"Wait a minute. Wait a minute." Rizzoli says. "So we are all supposed to be jumping around like rabbits?"

"Speak for yourself, Rabbit."

"What if I don't go along with this?"

"Now Rizzoli," Eldridge says, "I belong here by being the more physical of the two of us. I shouldn't have to prove that by kicking your fat ass. Look at you. You'll be lucky to come out on top in the mailroom. You let yourself go to pot, Rizzoli."

Fat ass? What's he talking? Rizzoli glances down his necktie and suddenly senses he is newly ample in the waist. *What the . . .?* He stands up. *It's a potbelly!*

"You got to concede I'm the better man for this job," Eldridge continues, a bemused, confident smile on his face now. "My first real fight for this job will probably be Kongas, who is fourth on the organizational chart."

Something is going wrong this instant; Rizzoli doesn't know what until he reaches for his nose and feels—his eyeglasses have slipped. *Glasses? I'm wearing glasses??* He's never worn them before. He takes them off and Eldridge and the room instantly dissolve into a shimmering blur.

"You want to take Kongas on, Rizzoli?" the now shapeless Eldridge is saying. "You want to take us both on?"

Rizzoli puts the glasses back on and sees a sharp-edged Eldridge and room. *I've aged. WHAT THE . . .?*

"You really got to concede I'm the better man for the job," Eldridge continues. "I'm young, Rizzoli, but, you . . . you let yourself go to pot and you're starting to look your age."

"Look my age? What do you mean? How old do you think I am exactly?" Rizzoli throws out, fishing for the right answer.

"I know exactly how old you are," Eldridge answers. "I been peeking at the payroll records. You forty-five."

FORTY-FIVE! Rizzoli's mouth falls open. *I'VE NEVER BEEN A DAY OVER THIRTY-THREE in my ENTIRE LIFE . . . until today, when instantly, I'm forty-five? . . .* "The hell with this," Rizzoli says. "I'm not going to squabble for a lousy mail-room slot. I'll just leave Miles Company altogether."

"And leave your pension?" Eldridge asks.

"Pension?" Rizzoli asks, trying to be nonchalant.

"Rizzoli, you're forty-five. You got to face facts."

FACTS? Rizzoli can see no way out for the moment but to resign himself to these strange circumstances. So with Eldridge hurrying him, he cleans out his desk on the spot. With only the few personal belongings he thinks he'll need in the mailroom, he heads for the door.

"You be tough, my man," Eldridge says with a chuckle as Rizzoli waves dazedly and heads out the door and down the hallway. Around the corner, he sees Stoufolis, the old Greek who delivers coffee from the building's street-level diner.

"Hey, Rizzoli, I have to talk to you," Stoufolis says.

"Not now, Stoufolis, I'm too busy," Rizzoli says, knowing Stoufolis will talk his leg off if he stops. "Not now." Rizzoli is headed for the Personnel Department to check about his age and pension. *Yesterday when I was thirty-three. I could've cared less about a pension, and I'd rather have had the money but, now . . . TODAY?* It all makes Rizzoli suddenly sad. *This can't be.*

In the Personnel Office, Rizzoli asks his old friend Shirley to dispel his major doubts. He is secretly delighted to learn he was right all along about his birthdate and the current year. "Then I'm thirty-three," Rizzoli concludes.

"No, forty-five," Shirley says with utter seriousness. "You're trying not to admit your age, is all."

Rizzoli shows her how, subtracting, he gets thirty-three. She changes his result to forty-five. "Now stop this," she says. When Rizzoli insists, she fixes him with such a pitying look that Rizzoli drops it. "Just kidding, Ol' Shirl," he says. *Is this the New Math?*

Shirley goes on to tell him now that he's forty-five, he's vested in the pension plan. *VESTED?* Rizzoli hadn't ever given any serious thought to his pension plan before today. *My God, now that I'm vested, I can never leave Miles, can I?*

Rizzoli heads for the mailroom. Along the way, he again bypasses Stoufolis who is carrying a cardboard container of coffees and pastries. He beckons to Rizzoli futilely. Just outside the mailroom, Rizzoli readies himself to play king of the mountain with the weak, . . . old, and the just plain portly middle-aged ones like himself.

Immediately inside the door, Rizzoli comes face to face with none other than . . . *SHADELY!* Rizzoli curses his fate. *No, no! This can't be!* Rizzoli shrieks to himself. *Why this, God? Anything, anything but this. God! ANYTHING!*

Rizzoli is in utter shock as he sees a Shadely who is not a day over twenty-eight, the age both he and Rizzoli were when they first came to Miles. *I can't stand this,* Rizzoli thinks, looking at this fresh-faced Shadely who, clearly, is trim and in great shape. *From jogging? Maybe the Nautilus? The worm.*

On seeing Rizzoli, Shadely sneers and says, "So, you *have* gone to pot—it's true."

Rizzoli is crushed. *The snake! He wouldn't have dared say that to me yesterday.* Rizzoli vows he'll get even, somehow.

"I challenge Rizzoli," Rizzoli hears a voice say, somewhere in the mailroom. *Is it Mr. Whittaker?* Rizzoli wonders. It is. The Company President of only yesterday now challenges Rizzoli to an arm wrestle for rank in the mailroom.

"All right," says Rizzoli. They arm wrestle and Mr. Whittaker pins Rizzoli, who, still thinking of Whittaker as his boss, gives in, not wanting to humiliate the ex-president further.

Now Shadely steps in to challenge Whittaker to a wrestling match. "Whoever wins will be head of the mailroom," Shadely says, confidently. The two wrestle. Quickly, Shadely gets the old man down and pins his arm behind his back. "You give?"

Old Whittaker just grunts as Shadely applies more pressure. "Give?"

"I give."

This angers Rizzoli. He challenges Shadely, but Shadely quickly gets Rizzoli to give, too. It is Rizzoli's greatest humiliation. Shadely is head of the mailroom; Rizzoli is a mailroom boy along with Mr. Whittaker. Shadely is clearly pleased to be over them both, for once. *Fucking Shadely.*

Rizzoli vows to jog.

A memo arrives from the new General Manager and Rizzoli reads it before he hands it to Shadely:

February 12

To: Head of the Mailroom
From: Eldridge Driscoll, General Manager
Re: Five-Year Company Projection Schedule

Dear Chump,
Get this stuff to me quick or your ass is grass.

Eldridge

"Okay, Whittaker," Shadely says, "what I want from you are sales and production figures for the next five years."

"That's a great deal of work," Whittaker answers.

"Listen, Whittaker," Shadely says, "I want this mailroom to be the best mailroom in all of Axis International. Even if we no longer have what it takes to lead this company, we must be proud that we still have our own small part to play in the great future destiny of this company."

"For these kinds of salaries?" Whittaker asks, looking at a sheet. "Rizzoli and I take home $99.40 per week. You get $122.38."

Shadely smiles.

The bastard, Rizzoli thinks. *If only I had the pension already, I could tell him off here and now.*

"How do they expect us to live on that?" Whittaker asks. "I could get more on welfare."

"But your pride," Shadely says. "Think of your pride. Here you can take pride in what you do. Doing projections doesn't compare with kicking ass, but it *is* work."

"Besides," Shadely continues, forgetting his present status for the moment, "think of how your taxes and mine are going straight into the pockets of welfare chiselers." He goes on and on, working himself into a lather.

Finally, the work of the mailroom gets underway. Mr. Whittaker finishes the five-year projections, and Shadely takes credit for it. Time passes. *Days? Months?* Rizzoli doesn't know for sure. He just works and does nothing else. *Don't want to lose that pension,* he thinks. There's a side of himself he loves that tells Rizzoli, *Why sweat a pension?* His other, serious side answers, *Why? It's the future.*

———

Rizzoli is perched high up on a hard seat in the hot, smoky company gymnasium, next to Mr. Whittaker. All around them on the same wooden bleachers, is a noisy crowd of Miles Company employees, ready to watch a fight in the ring way down in the center of the gymnasium. The ring has red ropes and "MILES" is printed in red letters on the white canvas.

Rizzoli doesn't know who will be fighting, but he can

sense it's a big fight from the mood of the crowd. *I should know. Why don't I know??* Rizzoli wonders. But, rather than embarrass himself by asking, Rizzoli decides to wait and see. He has the feeling he's been with Miles a long time, but he can't be sure how long. *Years? Months? Maybe only a day more.*

The two robed fighters are in their respective corners, with their hoods up and heads down. Rizzoli can't see who the fighters are as the announcer steps up to the microphone that is hanging down in the middle of the ring.

"Tonight, Ladies and Gentlemen, you will witness the Miles Challenge Fight for Company President between two outstanding fighters. In this corner, wearing white trunks, weighing two hundred nineteen pounds, the current Marketing Vice-President and challenging for the title of President, Eldridge 'The Hammer' Driscoll!"

ELDRIDGE? For PRESIDENT?

Eldridge slips off his robe and dances into the center of the ring, shadow-boxing, as the crowd breaks into applause.

"And now, in the red corner, weighing two hundred twenty-two pounds, the current Production Vice-President and challenging for President, Wayne 'The Sledge' Shadely!"

SHADELY? NO! Rizzoli is beside himself. Shadely slips his robe off. Rizzoli can't believe this is really Shadely, *but, it is, only he hasn't aged a bit in all the time that's passed. And look at me! He's still twenty-eight years old and I must be . . . fifty? Even when we were both twenty-eight he wasn't gigantic like that! When did he put on the bulk and the muscle,* Rizzoli wonders, truly astonished.

Gracefully weaving, with his lithe muscles rippling in waves, Shadely shadow boxes a fast furious ten seconds in his corner.

Rizzoli is aroused to partisan passion. *The Snake has to be stopped. Eldridge will do it. Come on, Eldridge. ELDRIDGE? FOR PRESIDENT? YES! YES! ELDRIDGE!* Rizzoli notes that Eldridge has a killer sense—something about him. He wants this *bad.*

With the fight just about to start, Rizzoli is agitated. he runs his hand through his hair. *WHAT? NO HAIR ON TOP! I'M BALDING? How old am I??* The sight of the young Shadely tensed in his corner with a full head of black hair sickens Rizzoli. *DO HIM IN, ELDRIDGE BABY.*

The referee brings both fighters to the center of the ring, gives them instructions, and sends them back to their corners to wait for the bell. Rizzoli is on the edge of his seat. The bell rings for the first round.

The fighters come out, weaving, jabbing, dancing, feeling one another out. Eldridge lets loose with a sudden quick combination—jabs and a hard right uppercut that catches Shadely coming in. Shadely wobbles and Rizzoli instantly senses he is hurt. Eldridge moves in, smelling blood, snapping Shadely's head back with lightning-fast jackhammer left jabs. "Stop the Snake," Rizzoli implores, as Eldridge lands a right and a left. Shadely drops to the canvas.

"E-L-L-L-LDRI-I-I-I-D-G-E, B-A-ABY!" Rizzoli suddenly screams out, leaping to his feet. "THAT'S MY MAN. FINISH HIM OFF!" Only now does Rizzoli realize the rest of the Miles crowd is dead quiet, and even Mr. Whittaker is embarrassed for him.

"Rizzoli," Mr. Whittaker whispers, "the Miles crowd

doesn't like to show any partisan feelings until a clear winner is in sight, so wait for the referee's count before cheering our fighter Eldridge."

The referee's count gets to seven, and Rizzoli can see the crowd is swayed over to Eldridge, ready to cheer him lustily. Then Shadely gets up, wobbly, at the count of eight. Rizzoli observes the crowd is swayed back to fence-straddling silence.

Eldridge quickly closes for the kill and lands a right. Shadely counters with a lightning series of left hooks and right crosses. He surprises Eldridge. *No*, Rizzoli thinks. *No*. A hard Shadely right to the jaw sends Eldridge's mouthpiece flying, and he's hurt, staggering backwards as Shadely swarms him with jabs and hard rights. Eldridge is down. He's up at the count of eight. A hard jab. He's down again. The referee is counting over him.

Now that a clear winner might be in sight, Rizzoli notices that the whole crowd (*with the exception of me and Mr. Whittaker here*) is uniformly shouting, "Shadely, Shadely, Shadely." *They just want a SURE Winner. They'll cheer any SURE WINNER*, Rizzoli thinks, as he hears Mr. Whittaker whisper, "I should have fired that Shadely long ago." "You sure should have," Rizzoli whispers back to him.

The crowd leaps to its feet, cheering loudly. The referee is holding Shadely's hand up high, victorious, and the announcer is saying, "The new President of Miles Company with a knockout in two minutes, twenty-two seconds in the first round, Wayne 'The Sledge' Shadely."

Rizzoli is dumbfounded. Finally, he joins the crowd by

standing up but is aghast that his potbelly has become a gut. *What the . . .?*

Rizzoli's attention is diverted as Mr. Whittaker confides, "Sad, but no surprise really that Shadely would win this fight. It's the steroids make him hit like that."

"Steroids?" Rizzoli asks, not at all surprised, knowing there's nothing Shadely wouldn't do to win.

"Rumor has been around forever about Shadely and steroids," Mr. Whittaker tells Rizzoli. "The Heads of Axis know it. But they never bother to check him out. They like what Shadely can do. Well, back to the mailroom, Rizzoli, huh?"

Rizzoli has spied Stoufolis across the crowd, and he watches the Greek collect a bet from someone in Quality Control. He can't believe a third person favored Eldridge enough before the fight to lay a bet. *And the Greek sniffed out the poor devil*, Rizzoli thinks, shaking his head and laughing to himself. "Back to the mailroom, Mr. Whittaker."

———

For days? Weeks? Months? Rizzoli does nothing else but work in the mailroom alongside old Mr. Whittaker. Out of consideration, Rizzoli lets the old guy run the operation, thinking, *Even though I could take him.*

Meanwhile, almost every week Rizzoli, on his rounds delivering office mail, hears news that Miles Company President Shadely has knocked out another Axis International Division Head in some distant city. Shadely's rise to power within Axis soon becomes so spectacular that even Rizzoli has to wonder, *Who is there to take the snake*? Then Rizzoli hears that Shadely has done the ultimate.

"You mean Shadely beat Peter MacArthur III, Chairman of the Board? The Chicago guy who instituted the big change in the first place?" Rizzoli asks Shirley in Personnel.

"It's *Mr.* Shadely," Shirley corrects him.

Rizzoli can't bear to insert "Mr." before that snake's name, so he just smiles pleasantly at Shirley.

"And don't sound so incredulous, Rizzoli. Yes, *our* Mr. Shadely triumphed over MacArthur. It was inevitable."

Inevitable? Rizzoli stops smiling. He can only shake his head and leave to deliver the office mail. Shadely is now at the pinnacle; it makes Rizzoli weary to think of it.

I'd quit now if I had my pension. PENSION? It makes Rizzoli even wearier to think of the power the pension has over him. *If only I weren't vested, I could leave. WHAT AM I THINKING?*

A little while later (Rizzoli is not sure how little time *really passed—a year? A day?*), he gets a summons upstairs to see *Shadely.* It seems Shadely, as the new Axis Chairman of the Board, is passing through New York City inspecting the Miles Division where he recently installed a new "tough puppet," someone, in Rizzoli's words, "to be the Head Cheese at Miles."

Rizzoli is nervous and hurries to meet Shadely when he runs into Stoufolis, who wants to chat. "Not now," Rizzoli says in passing, certain the Greek wants to talk about the horse races and which jockey looks good. "Not now."

Inside Mr. Whittaker's old office the new executive secretary, a well-muscled redhead named Ray, motions

Rizzoli in. She says, "He's expecting you, Rizzoli."

Rizzoli enters the inner office, sees *HIM* and says, "Hello, Shadely."

"*Mr.* Shadely," Shadely says, matter-of-factly. "*Mr.* Shadely."

Shadely is still twenty-eight years old with a full head of black hair and this greatly disappoints Rizzoli. Shadely seems even more powerfully built than he did the night he pulverized Eldridge.

Looking at Shadely standing there, Rizzoli has a flashback to when they were both twenty-eight. *I could have taken Shadely with one hand tied to my leg back then when we were both 160 pounds,* Rizzoli thinks. *I could have taken him any way. Any day.*

"Rizzoli, I hardly recognized you," Shadely says, not extending his hand to shake, just standing, sizing up Rizzoli. "When did your hair turn white?"

WHITE HAIR? ME? Rizzoli is completely distracted when Shadely says, "Well, enough catching up, Rizzoli, let me get right to the point. I'm a busy man."

Shadely proceeds to inform Rizzoli that Rizzoli is now only weeks away from age sixty, when he'll get his pension.

Rizzoli manages a little smile. Then he looks at Shadely with his dark hair and is furious at the injustice of it.

"Your pension is yours, Rizzoli."

Good. Then I'm out of here, Rizzoli thinks.

"If you can outbox the new man I'm bringing in to compete for that last mailroom slot of yours. Stankovich is his name, but he likes people to call him 'Mad Dog'."

Rizzoli chokes; he is suddenly enraged.

"Your fight is set for this week." Shadely adds, "Oh, and Whittaker can be in on it too. We'll make it a round-robin tournament—you, old man Whittaker and 'Mad Dog.'"

Rizzoli can't utter a word; he gasps and sputters and wants to leap across the table at Shadely's throat.

"I want more power in that mailroom now that I have Axis ready and mobilized for The Great Merger Wars. You understand, I'm sure, Rizzoli."

Rizzoli glares at Shadely who—all business now—concludes by saying, "Incidentally, I recently made all company pensions arbitrary, so even if you or Whittaker should win the round-robin, I wouldn't want anyone thinking he has automatic pension rights. You've got your work cut out for you. Good Luck."

Rizzoli's anger is so great he's already up and stomping out, through Shadely's reception area and into the outdoor hallway. He's so furious he's almost blinded when he hears, "Rizzoli, my old pal, hey, what makes you so angry?"

It's Stoufolis. Rizzoli tells him what just happened in a tense, shaking voice. Rizzoli can only think of getting revenge.

"Rizzoli, listen to me. I can help you," Stoufolis says. "Who do you think has been giving steroids to Shadely?"

Rizzoli listens intently.

"I give him steroids," says Stoufolis, "but, to you I'll give something even stronger."

Stronger? YES! Rizzoli can only think of getting back at Shadely. *I'll show the snake.*

"With this," Stoufolis says, opening his palm and letting Rizzoli glimpse a single white pill, "you will topple Shadely and lead Axis. No one can challenge you within Axis, Incorporated, or, without. You will conquer all."

"I will beat Shadely, you say, Stoufolis?"

"Guaranteed, Rizzoli. You and I can set the round even, and I can win us some big money on the side."

"Guaranteed?" Rizzoli can't believe it.

"Listen, Shadely is nothing. Axis will dominate with you in power," Stoufolis continues. "Axis will conquer Rexall Drugs, the Federal Food and Drug Administration, Russia, the world."

Rizzoli isn't really listening to all of this; he just wants to beat Shadely so badly he could die.

"Under your rule, Axis will have the world's greatest air force and navy, and its salesmen will be great soldiers," Stoufolis says, all worked up now. "Think of it, Rizzoli. All rival companies will fall. Non-related industries will capitulate. The federal regulatory agencies will do Axis' bidding. The UN will pass laws drafted by Axis. Are you listening to me, Rizzoli?"

Rizzoli isn't listening: instead, he has become intent on imagining his hand being raised in triumph by the referee as Shadely lies sprawled on the canvas, crushed by Rizzoli's blows.

"Here, then, Rizzoli," Stoufolis says, "all you do is take this." He hands Rizzoli the pill. "It's the only one I have."

"But what do *you* want out of this?" Rizzoli asks, ready to take the pill.

"Rizzoli, what you can give me is simple: your pension. I will give you a better pension. A pension of limitless duration, not the measly Axis pension. A fine pension that guarantees you life everlasting under my care."

Everlasting? Suddenly Rizzoli is utterly terrified to think how close he has just come to making this pact with . . . ? He thinks of the letter beginning the first name. Then Rizzoli blurts out, "Listen, I wasn't born yesterday, Stoufolis. I know who you are."

Stoufolis says . . . "What are you talking about, Rizzoli?"

"I'm on to you," Rizzoli says, and, with all the pent-up anger he has at Shadely, he yells, "BETTER I CROAK ON SOCIAL SECURITY WITHOUT ANY PENSION THAN BE A SUPER, SUPER SHADELY AND YOUR SLAVE FOREVER!"

"So croak on Social Security, Rizzoli," Stoufolis yells back, holding his ground. "You and Social Security don't belong in this twentieth century of limitless power."

This commotion out in the hall causes Shadely to come out screaming, obviously having heard the whole conversation between Rizzoli and Stoufolis. "Get out of here NOW, Rizzoli," Shadely says. "YOU'RE FIRED!"

"My pleasure," says Rizzoli. He starts down the hallway and instantly he feels free: free from the pension, no longer vested. *My own man again,* he thinks. Behind him, he hears Shadely say to Stoufolis, "We have something to talk about, you and I."

Rizzoli ducks into the men's room, goes into a stall ,and tosses the pill into a toilet bowl. He will get his revenge on Shadely after all. He flushes it. *Shadely'll just have to make do with steroids, and not the Ultimate.*

Rizzoli feels he has won a great victory but he knows there's another battle to come. He leaves the stall and passes in front of the men's room mirror going out. He is an old man now, and proud of it. He has very thick glasses . . . liver spots . . . lines . . . and a white mustache. He accepts himself looking so very, very old. *I'm my own man now, no longer vested.*

Rizzoli looks at himself a long while before going out to do what he has to do. He won't delude himself; he refuses to run. He imagines waves of youth coming at him, one wave replenished by another, overwhelming an old man. It's inevitable. Rizzoli knows the score.

RIZZOLI DREAMS "Rizzoli. What? You living in this
HE SETTLES A neighborhood now?" Rizzoli hears
LONG-STANDING someone holler outside his favor-
ACCOUNT WITH THE ite Greek diner on Amster-
MAN OF PROPERTY dam. Rizzoli turns and sees
him a few feet away. *No, not him,* Rizzoli thinks. *The
Man of Property.* Rizzoli barely knows him, and they
only occasionally run into each other.

"Yeah, I've been living in this neighborhood a good
while now," Rizzoli says. "Must be five years. I was living here when I last saw you, a couple of years ago. I
told you then."

"Yeah, where you livin'? What street?"

"75th."

"Between?"

"Columbus and the Park," Rizzoli answers. Now
Rizzoli anticipates he'll say: "Good block."

"Good block. You own or rent?"

Humhead has to ask that question every time, Rizzoli
thinks. *Every time! It's been years, but still, it being him, I
can't believe I wasn't ready for it.* Smiling faintly, Rizzoli
searches his mind for a comeback to put this guy in his
place, once and for all. But the question has irritated
him so much he can't unscramble his mind.

"Still rent, huh?" The Man of Property concludes.

No. Calm yourself. Tell him you PREFER *renting. I do,*
Rizzoli thinks, *but why should I tell that to shmuck here?*
Rizzoli finally asks, "What?"

The Man of Property doesn't bother repeating the
question. A little smile breaks across his face as he

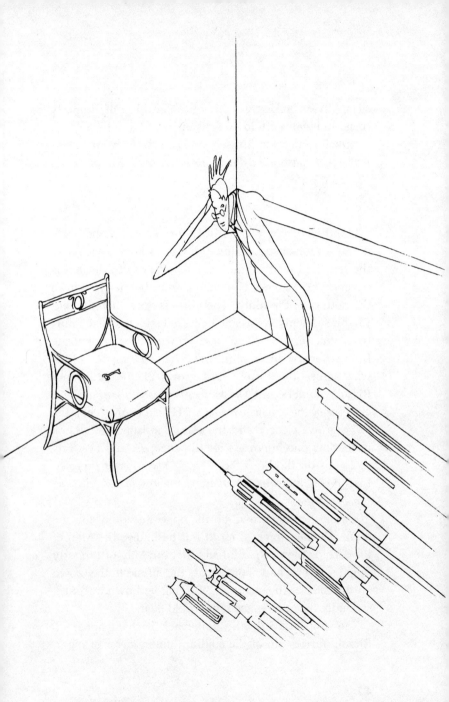

says, "Well, take care, Rizzoli." The Man of Property turns and walks off down Amsterdam.

Rizzoli is angry at himself. *Shmuck thinks he can define me by that question! Just wait, Property Man,* Rizzoli vows, *Just wait.*

———————

Months later on a beautiful afternoon at Yankee Stadium, Rizzoli sits watching a three-run homer arch over the left field wall as Yankee fans erupt with deafening cheers. The Yankees have come from behind to win in the bottom of the ninth. The noise is overwhelming but Rizzoli suddenly swears he hears a distinct voice coming from that faraway third base crowd, directly opposite from where he sits behind first. The voice carries all the way across the infield and grows clearer still until Rizzoli wonders, *Is it The Man of Property talking at someone over by the opponent's dugout?* He isn't sure. Then the voice grows clearer and the tone unmistakable: "Look in the low one hundreds for the cheapest and best buy in co-ops on the West Side . . . ." *The Man of Property,* Rizzoli concludes, *is over there giving unsolicited advice to some poor fan.*

Rizzoli eyes the crowd on the opposite side of the stadium. He can't pick him out but he knows the Man of Property is there. Rizzoli fears that the Man of Property might spot him and shout across the infield to the crowd on this side of the stadium, "Rizzoli, you own or rent?" so loudly that all Yankee fans would hear.

Knowing he'd have no comeback if that happened, Rizzoli hurries out of the stadium under cover of night, vowing to pick the moment for his comeback. *You wait, Property Man.*

––––––––

"Condos are scarce on Sutton Place compared to co-ops and that's what makes condos there such a good investment . . . the price per square foot," the Man of Property is telling someone, 'The price per square foot."

It's HIS voice, Rizzoli concludes. *No mistaking it this time.*

Months have gone by since Yankee Stadium, and Rizzoli has forgotten all about the Man of Property. Rizzoli stares at his TV, which is showing a live broadcast of the Democratic Convention from a southern city hundreds of miles outside of New York. As the camera pans the sea of delegates on the floor of the huge Convention Center, Rizzoli tries to spot The Man of Property. He can't. Yet, from the noisy, excited crowd shown on the small screen, Rizzoli still overhears that loud, clear, unmistakable voice talking to another conventioneer. Rizzoli peers at the tiny, indistinct convention faces. He switches tactics, deciding to look first for a tiny convention face so bored it could shriek at having to listen. *And right next to that face will be the Man of Property.*

Suddenly, the TV camera zooms in on the New York delegation and then zooms closer and closer until the whole screen is filled with the face of the Man of Property, but with no sound.

It makes Rizzoli anxious to have the Man of Property perched there, soundlessly. Rizzoli thinks, *Any moment,*

he just might ask me, live from the Democratic Convention,
"Hey, Rizzoli, you own or rent?" Rizzoli turns the TV off.
Just to be safe, you never know. "You just wait!" Rizzoli
suddenly screams at his dead TV. "I'm ready for you,
Property Man."

———

Months pass. Rizzoli is coming out of the Greek diner,
his head down.

"Rizzoli."

Rizzoli looks up. It's the Man of Property. He has a
worried look, as if something unexpected has happened
to him.

"Maybe you heard," says the Man of Property. "I've
been in the hospital."

Rizzoli shakes his head.

"I got a new heart, virtually" says the Man of Property proudly. "New ventricles, new valves."

"So," says Rizzoli, "do you own or rent?"

RIZZOLI GETS
THE INSIDE STORY
FROM A CABBIE Rizzoli sees only the back of the cabbie's square head. His eyes, though, are reflected in the rearview mirror, and they are looking back at Rizzoli.

"You're right," the cabbie says, "they sure do leave a lot of them umbrellas in here. Sometimes I look back and see a guy's umbrella and he's already outside the cab walking away after he pays his fare. So I tap on the window, but he don't hear. I can chase after him, sure, but this here's New York and, sure, I get him his umbrella, but meanwhile the schmo in the car behind me has pushed *my* cab into the East River. This here's New York—you get my drift?"

"Got you," Rizzoli says.

"So them there umbrellas pile up over time. I got 'em all in my garage. I go off shift, drive home, park the cab in the garage and start to empty out the back seat. Umbrellas! Some days I got two, three, four umbrellas to leave in the garage. You should *see* my garage. Umbrellas up the wazoo! So I'm always buying some tool I already got two, three of 'cause I couldn't find the one I was looking for, cause it was buried under all them umbrellas, if you get my meaning."

"Got it," Rizzoli says. "You got umbrellas."

"Umbrellas! And them ladies! I don't know what possesses them ladies, but one'll be sitting there all dressed up and sure as shit she'll start taking off her outta garments. First one glove, then the other. She'll leave 'em right there on the seat, in a pile, neat-like. So I got tons of them ladies' gloves. And them scarves and such. To go with them umbrellas. I tell you, it's getting near impossible to find a freakin' tool in my garage. You get

my drift, don't ya?"

"You need a tool and it's the last thing you're going to find," Rizzoli says.

"You got it, all right. You got it right there, pal. So guess what I got planned for this here three-day weekend?"

Rizzoli shakes his head; he can't imagine.

"I'm cleaning the garage," says the cabbie, glancing in the rearview mirror to see if the guy he's got in the back is an idiot, or what? "And guess what I got planned after that?" the cabbie asks.

"What?" Rizzoli says, distracted. *Remember to get a receipt.*

"A yard sale."

"A what?"

"A yard sale. To peddle all them gloves and scarves and umbrellas and them tools I got two, three, even four of."

"I got you," Rizzoli says, fumbling for change.

The cab pulls to the curb and stops. Rizzoli pays his fare, gets the receipt, and starts off. Then he stops: *I left my umbrella!* He looks back and sees the cabbie tapping the window. The cabbie waves. *No, I didn't bring an umbrella. Did I?* He smiles at the cabbie, waves back, turns, and walks on.

THE DREAM OF MRS. LUNDY INTRODUCING HER MALE FRIENDS TO RIZZOLI Rizzoli dreams he is sitting on his own brown couch, in a lobby with a revolving door leading out to the sidewalk. Mrs. Lundy sits directly opposite him in a brown chair that matches the couch. Together, through the big plate glass window, they are watching people pass by on the street.

"I met a good friend of mine the other day," Mrs. Lundy says, smiling, still watching the street. "I want to introduce you two. I know you'll enjoy him."

Rizzoli smiles. It's so nice, just him and Mrs. Lundy. She is his one real friend. They are comfortable with each other; Rizzoli feels no need to hide anything from her. "You know me inside and out," Rizzoli has told her on occasion.

"Rizzoli, did you hear?"

"I did. That would be nice."

Out she goes through the revolving door. Back she comes through the revolving door with her friend.

She introduces them.

"Chester. Rizzoli." She pauses, "Rizzoli. Chester."

Chester and Rizzoli shake hands.

Mrs. Lundy again sits in the brown chair. Chester sits in another brown chair next to her. Rizzoli sits across from the two of them on the big brown couch.

Wanting Rizzoli and Chester to be friends, Mrs. Lundy brings up many things she thinks they have in common. "You both hate to be caught in a downpour without an umbrella," she says. "You're both finicky about where to sit on a park bench."

Rizzoli is trying hard to like Chester, but the man sucks air between his teeth going "eeeth, eeeth," an irritating habit Rizzoli soon finds he can't stand. Rizzoli says nothing to Chester about it, of course, because that would embarrass Mrs. Lundy. Instead, he smiles and continues to try to make polite conversation. *I'll put up with Chester, if it means so much to Mrs. Lundy. But what does she see in him?* Rizzoli is certain he has little or nothing in common with Chester.

In the weeks afterward, Rizzoli continues to endure Chester, who frequently accompanies Mrs. Lundy when she comes to see Rizzoli. Rizzoli listens to Chester sucking air between his teeth until it nearly drives him mad, but he doesn't say anything.

One day Mrs. Lundy enters through the revolving door with a man Rizzoli has never seen before. "Rizzoli, this is Ben," she says. "Ben. Rizzoli." They shake. "Ben and I have been seeing one another for the past few weeks, and I told him that he had to be sure and meet you, Rizzoli, because you two would probably become instant friends. You're so alike," she tells them.

They sit in the two brown chairs, and Rizzoli sits on the couch opposite them.

As Rizzoli and Ben talk, Mrs. Lundy smiles first at one then the other. They talk about the weather and agree it might rain that afternoon. Rizzoli likes Ben. *At least he doesn't suck air like that last one.* They talk and begin to loosen up with one another.

". . . and sitting is necessary exercise, too," Rizzoli is saying.

"Jiminy Christmas, I hadn't thought of it that way,"

Ben says to Rizzoli.

". . . and standing is necessary exercise.. . ."

"Jiminy Christmas, of course."

". . . lying down . . ."

"Jiminy Christmas, you learn something new every day."

What's with him? Jiminy Christmas? Rizzoli gets to the point where he can't stand Ben saying it. Ben goes on saying it. One more time and Rizzoli is afraid that he'll punch him. Of course, he wouldn't because Mrs. Lundy would never forgive him for that. So Rizzoli keeps making conversation and smiling at Ben. *It's hard to make conversation when I have so little in common with him,* Rizzoli thinks.

Weeks go by. Rizzoli puts up with Ben saying "Jiminy Christmas." Finally, he wants to scream. Then, fortunately, Mrs. Lundy stops seeing Ben.

One day Mrs. Lundy enters the lobby alone. She sits on the brown couch with Rizzoli.

"Men! Agggh," she says to Rizzoli. "You get so you can't stand them sometimes. Did you ever notice how Chester sucked air between his teeth? I don't know how you could stand it."

"I couldn't," Rizzoli confesses. "But I wouldn't say anything. I was afraid I'd lose your friendship."

"That's sweet," Mrs. Lundy says.

Then they talk about Ben. It turns out that "Jiminy Christmas" drove her crazy, too. They laugh. Their conversation becomes animated. Their friendship is back to the way it used to be. *What good friends we are,* Rizzoli thinks.

"What would I do without you, Mrs. Lundy?" Rizzoli

asks.

"And what would I do without you?"

In the days afterward, they enjoy each other's company. Then one day Mrs. Lundy announces she has met a new man named Vincent; she says she wants Rizzoli to give her his honest impression of the guy right off.

Mrs. Lundy brings Vincent to meet Rizzoli. Vincent sits in the chair next to Mrs. Lundy. Rizzoli genuinely likes him. Rizzoli finds he has a lot in common with Vincent. *Vincent even looks a little like me,* Rizzoli thinks, deciding now to tell Mrs. Lundy his honest impressions. *After all, she has always shot straight with me. Why shouldn't I do the same for her?* With Vincent out of the room for a moment, Rizzoli tells her. Mrs. Lundy is glad. She is fond of Vincent.

When Vincent comes back, Rizzoli gets up and goes to the bathroom. As he comes back into the room, Rizzoli hears Vincent whisper, "Why does Rizzoli have to say, 'You know' all the time?"

This is the first time Rizzoli realizes he uses that expression.

"I don't know why," says Mrs. Lundy in a whisper. "But I know he always says 'You know' all the time."

"You were wrong," Vincent says. "He and I have little in common."

"Do you want to leave then?"

"Why don't we? If it's not too much bother."

When Rizzoli sits down, they make an excuse and leave. In the days afterward, Rizzoli sits alone on the couch across from the two empty chairs and watches as the pages fall off the calendar, and a new calendar goes up.

One day Louie at the newsstand tells Rizzoli that Mrs. Lundy married and moved away.

"Who'd she marry?" Rizzoli asks. "That guy Vincent?"

"Vincent. That was it. The one who said 'you know' all the time."

"He did?" Rizzoli asks.

"You never noticed that?"

"No."

"You couldn't have been with him two minutes and not notice it. Maybe you didn't spend enough time with him. Maybe that was it."

"That was it."

RIZZOLI DREAMS (A dreaming Rizzoli finds himself
HE FINALLY UNDERSTANDS in total darkness. All
THE FORGOTTEN PROFESSOR'S he knows is that in
FAVORITE CONCEPT every direction he looks, it is
totally black. He can't even see if he has a body; he
thinks he does, but he can't be sure—it's so black, pitch
black. He wonders if that is his hand really touching his
leg, or if he just thinks he has a hand and a leg. He
doesn't think he is alone, since in the distance he seems
to hear low voices. But he can't be sure. Suddenly,
nearby, sound erupts. Rizzoli jumps, startled to hear
someone's loud voice.)

A Voice: You have the basic New York draw. Nothing
more, and nothing less.

Rizzoli: *(What? What'd he say?)* Huh? *(Is that voice
close? Or coming over a loudspeaker? Or what?)*
Huh?

A Voice: Your draw is The Reverse Paradigm with New
York City. I'm going to explain the situation to
you *once.* So, listen.

Rizzoli: *(The what? Paradigm? It's, it's that visiting professor I had at NYU Summer Session that one
year. Plottsman? Plottsberg? Plottstein? Plotts?
"Reverse Paradigm" did he say? I never did get
the "reverse" one, and now I've even forgotten
his use of the word "paradigm." Damn.)*

The Forgotten Professor: Listen. I don't want any interruptions until I'm through explaining the situation that you are now confronting as a result
of your draw. Then I'll answer questions for a
set period. Do you understand?

Rizzoli: *(Is Plotts talking to me? Where am I? Plotts sounds exactly like he used to when he gave instructions for his exams.)*

The Forgotten Professor: NO INTERRUPTIONS. (A long pause.) You drew New York City and beat tremendous odds. Many people wish they had your draw instead of their own. (A sudden murmur of other voices in the darkness.)

Rizzoli: *(Others are here? He's not talking to me? I'm a New Yorker already. He's talking to one of them. Who are the others? What are their draws?)*

The Forgotten Professor: A New York City draw is the good part. (Pause) There's more. This is crucial. Listen. You have to take your chances on what you're going to get when you show up down there. If you actually make good on your draw and go down there.

Rizzoli: *(Go down to New York City? From where? Where the fuck is this? LIMBO? Ask Professor Plotts where this is. Speak up! No, No, make sure it's Plotts first. Plotts? No, that's not it.)*

The Forgotten Professor: You go down there, you could wind up a Wall Street broker. Or a hard drug addict, or a bread truck driver.

Rizzoli: *(Junkie?)*

The Forgotten Professor: You simply don't know. It's potluck. You might even wind up a philosophy professor.

Rizzoli: *(Is it Plottstein? Speak up. Say, "Excuse me there, Professor Plottstein, where are we right here now? Plottstein? No, that's not it at all. Stotts? Professor Stotts?)*

The Forgotten Professor: You don't know, PERIOD. Beforehand there's no way of knowing *who*
you're going to be, *what* you'll do for a living,
how you'll make it from day to day. That's the
choice you make. That's the chance you take.
But there are many men who would do anything for that chance to be on Wall Street
even though overwhelming odds say they are
more likely to wind up poor, black, and female, in say, Brownsville or Bedford-
Stuyvesant. That's the chance you take.

Rizzoli: *(Did he say a female? EVERYTHING IS CHANCE?*
But at least get straight where we are right now.
Ask the Professor. No. No, you're going to draw
attention to yourself when he's not talking to you
anyway.)

The Forgotten Professor: You show up down there and
only then do you find out the essentials: who
your parents are, if you have any; your job, if
you have one; your skin color; if you have
money or not; the web of your existence.
Now there's more. This is crucial. You go
down and you show up *immediately.* IMMEDI-
ATELY, you understand? You show up immediately as a twenty-one year old. How do
people there NOT REALIZE you haven't been
there for twenty-one years previous? THEY
DON'T, PERIOD. WHY? They don't know any
difference because that's the way the situation you drew works out. They THINK you
have been there, in their family, twenty-one
years growing up. They don't know any dif-

ference. They're what we call "deluded." They have compelling delusions. We lace their minds with memories of you stretching back for twenty-one years. So, if it's a family, say, they think you've been there in their family twenty-one years growing up. And you think so, too. This is crucial because you're what we call deluded too. You think you really grew up in this family. Your friends do. Everybody who knows you has quote memories quote of you. You just showed up but you possess a whole life in your quote memory quote. You don't know the difference. You're deluded. If you're a hard drug addict, there's twenty-one years of your quote memories quote of why you're a social deviant. Or, if you're on Wall Street, to use another example, you have your quote memories quote of college, law school—the whole web of that particular existence.

Rizzoli: *(Web?)*

The Forgotten Professor: And documents. We have them flawlessly forged and in place: college transcripts, prison records, whatever. Everything is in place for your new life: documents, memories, all strands of an existence.

Rizzoli: *(It's coming back to me now. All those notes I took that summer when Philosophy was the only offering to fill the requirement. "Existence, Freedom and The Ultimate Paradigm"—that was the course title! And he was Professor Stotts? Stippleman? Ipple? Bibble?? It'll come to me. At any* rate he's not talking to me. He's talking to these others who are not New Yorkers. They have to have a way to fit in, so somebody thought this up—maybe.)

The Forgotten Professor: So, if you go down, that's *your* choice. Nobody can make it for you. You make the choice, and then it's a straight gamble where you're going to land. You might get lucky. You play the odds in the basic New York Draw . . .

Rizzoli: *(Am I wrong? But didn't someone once tell me this professor loved betting the trotters at Roosevelt?)*

The Forgotten Professor: Now let me sum things up. You aren't going to be you . . . *if* you go down there. You're going to be whoever you become down there. Listen. If you want to be *you*, you stay *here*, in the dark.

Rizzoli: *(WHAT? Wait a minute here! To be ME, I have to stay here? MY ASS! I'm a New Yorker already. I don't have to play some diddly squat game in the dark.)*

The Forgotten Professor: What I just presented you is the ultimate freedom of existence in The Reverse Paradigm. It's the supreme existential question. Being or being. The risk of freedom in the dark or the light, as you or another.

Rizzoli: *(That's right out of his notes, "The Reverse Existential Paradigm." "Being or being." The RE-VERSE PARADIGM was Plott's favorite concept, but it was too abstract. I never got a real sense of it, until now.)*

The Forgotten Professor: So if you want to go down I
        can't guarantee you a thing but I can give you
        odds on being on Wall Street.
Rizzoli: *(WALL STREET?)*
The Forgotten Professor: Being Armenian, living in
        Chelsea, being blind, being a prostitute, male
        or female, a heroin addict, you name it. If it's
        in New York, I can quote you odds. (Pause) So
        now, in closing, I'm going to answer any
        questions you might have.
Rizzoli: Listen, I just want to check something out,
        Professor. I'm Rizzoli and that's not who
        you're talking to, is it? I'm not supposed to be
        . . . *(in this class, am I?)* . . . here, Am I? I'm
        already a New Yorker, that's Rizzoli, R-I-Z-Z-
        0-L-I.
The Forgotten Professor: Rizzoli. R-I-Z-Z-0-L-I.
Rizzoli: Yes, that's me. Incidentally, I think I took a
        course from you at NYU one summer, years
        ago. You were a visiting professor?
The Forgotten Professor: No. I never taught at NYU.
Rizzoli: *(He's forgotten. But his name is Plotts, I know.
        Ask him if that's it. Plotts?)* I could have sworn,
        but then . . . *(I remember now how incredibly
        forgetful this guy was. Ipple? Professor Ipple? Ip-
        pleman. Stipple?)*
The Forgotten Professor: To answer your question,
        everybody here was already a New Yorker
        but only you drew New York and got what
        they all wanted, Rizzoli. You're lucky. So why
        don't you tell me what you're aiming for, if
        you go down, and I'll give you odds on it.

Rizzoli: Single. Mid-thirties. Italian. Apartment on West 75th. Median income. Decent job.

The Forgotten Professor: Italian? On the Upper West Side. You'll have much better odds on being Italian in say, Bensonhurst, Staten Island even. Upper West Side? Maybe you want to be Jewish? You'd have better odds on getting that neighborhood if you're thinking Jewish.

Rizzoli: I like Jews . . .

The Forgotten Professor: You don't have to like Jews to wind up a Jew, Rizzoli. It's odds we're talking. Chance. Straight chance.

Rizzoli: *(The Professor doesn't think I'm dumb, does he?)*

The Forgotten Professor: New York odds are good on being Jewish—better Jewish than Italian in that certain neighborhood.

Rizzoli: All right, what are the odds on what I said I'm shooting for? Italian. Upper West Side.

The Forgotten Professor: 1,684,203,389 to one.

Rizzoli: To get my old life back, that's what I described to you.

The Forgotten Professor: That's the hardest thing of all, the longest odds of all. Odds on just being a white male are 64,320 to one. Most of them are in the suburbs.

Rizzoli: I go to sleep, Professor *(Stotts?)*, I'm a certain New Yorker. I wake up and I have to take my chances on being *any* New Yorker?

The Forgotten Professor: Exactly.

Rizzoli: That doesn't seem fair.

The Forgotten Professor: Everybody here has a fair

chance. You're ahead of everybody else to begin with anyway.

Rizzoli: *[He thinks I'm AHEAD?]*

The Forgotten Professor: You drew New York instead of say, Newark or South Philly—some stark, forgotten wasteland offering no chance of being on Wall Street.

Rizzoli: *[WALL STREET? Who cares?]*

The Forgotten Professor: WASP? Would you like to be a WASP? White, wealthy, good education?

Rizzoli: *[No. I just want to be Rizzoli and in New York City, like before.]*

The Forgotten Professor: 63,647 to one on your being a WASP. The odds are high because most of them are in the suburbs, thus making a WASP a long shot in the City.

Rizzoli: Huh? *[The Professor really loves having all these exact odds.]*

The Forgotten Professor: Maybe you're looking for something different? Poor, black, single mother in Bedford-Stuyvesant. Good odds.

Rizzoli: *[WHAT?]*

The Forgotten Professor: 1682 to one on that one. I never know what somebody's looking for. So, what's it with you, Rizzoli? Besides getting your own life back—which is the greatest long shot of all—who would you like to be?

Rizzoli: *[Maybe I'll try somebody different.]* Black male, tenor or even an alto sax player in a good jazz trio.

The Forgotten Professor: 1,812,624 to one.

Rizzoli: *[It's a real CRAP SHOOT.]* I can stay here,

though, you said? Where is this anyway?

The Forgotten Professor: That's the one thing I can't tell you. Staying here in the dark *is* one of your choices, one side of The Reverse Paradigm.

Rizzoli: *(Those words again. They put me on edge . . .)*

The Forgotten Professor: Staying here isn't great, but at least you know you aren't a hard drug addict crawling around Times Square. Here in the dark at least you know you're you. So, what's it going to be? Here? Or New York City?

Rizzoli: *(Shit! I'm taking forever. I can't make up my mind.)*

The Forgotten Professor: Do you need any more odds? Puerto Rican in New York, 23,141 to one; French, 75,789 to one . . .

Rizzoli: *(Listen to him. How can I concentrate when I have this odds pedant yawping at me?)*

The Forgotten Professor: . . . Azerbajani, Kurdish, Moslem, Jewish, Southern Baptist, you name it. Sioux Indian? (A loudspeaker blares out an incomprehensible message.)

Rizzoli: *(It's the subway conductor.)* What's that?

The Forgotten Professor: That's the signal. Your time is up. You took too long. You didn't listen at the beginning when I told you, you had ten minutes from when I took questions.

Rizzoli: *(He forgot to give me full instructions at the beginning. And now he doesn't remember.)* Professor, you didn't tell me that at the beginning. I swear it.

The Forgotten Professor: That's it. You missed your
chance.

Rizzoli: WHAT? *(Asshole was this way when I tried to
             make up the midterm.)* WHAT, PROFESSOR? I
             WON'T STAND FOR THIS.

                    —Silence—

Rizzoli: NEVER. I WON'T STAND FOR THIS BULLSHIT!

                    —Silence—

Rizzoli: YOU CAN TAKE THIS LIMBO AND SHOVE IT UP
             YOUR *ASS*, PLOTTSTEIN!

                    —Silence—

Rizzoli: PISS ON YOUR LIMBO!

                    —Silence—

Rizzoli: WAIT A MINUTE. I'LL TAKE NEW YORK. I'LL BE
             HOMELESS, A JUNKY, A HOOKER—ANYTHING.

                    —Silence—

Rizzoli: ANYTHING.

                    —Silence—

RIZZOLI DREAMS OF AN EVERYDAY OCCURRENCE IN MIDTOWN MANHATTAN Rizzoli dreams he is walking along 42nd Street past Grand Central Station. Up ahead on the sidewalk, Rizzoli notices a muscular little guy in red satin boxing trunks marked *Everlast*. The little guy is sitting on a low stool. His neck and shoulders are being rubbed down from behind by an older bald guy who keeps up a chatter: "You can do it! Be tough! YOU CAN DO IT! GET 'EM!" He shoves paper into the boxer's hand, and the little guy suddenly jumps up and shouts "Here!" at an approaching businessman.

The businessman shakes his head.

"Here!" says the boxer. He jabs the flyer at him again.

"I don't want it."

"TAKE IT."

"No." The little guy left hooks the businessman, knocking him flat onto the sidewalk. He stuffs the flyer into the pocket of the businessman's grey flannel suit.

"ATTA BABY! ATTA BABY!" shouts the bald guy.

I'll just TAKE the flyer, Rizzoli decides as he approaches. He readies himself as the boxer approaches and says, "Here." *Smile. Take it.* Rizzoli tells himself. He will smile, and he will take it.

"HERE!"

Rizzoli's body won't obey him. He can't help himself. He stares right past the little guy. His face won't smile. His hand refuses to go out.

"ATTA BABY, ATTA BABY," Rizzoli hears in a daze, lying on the sidewalk. He feels a flyer being stuffed in his pocket.

"You got him," he hears the bald guy say.

RIZZOLI DREAMS OF BEING A CELEBRITY Rizzoli dreams that he gets up one morning, turns on the TV, and sees himself talking with the President of the United States. He has no recollection of ever having met the President but there he is saying, "Mr. President! The common man is the country's ace in the hole."

Rizzoli flips channels. To his surprise, he sees himself nearly everywhere. He turns the radio on, and hears his own voice, telling himself what's wrong with the economy. He listens and decides that he doesn't know anything about the economy. *But what am I doing telling others about the economy?* It doesn't make a difference to the interviewer: "What about the prime rate?" he asks Rizzoli, and Rizzoli answers. As Rizzoli flips the dial, he hears snatches of his own voice commenting on everything from aftershave to afterlife.

Rizzoli goes to the big wicker basket where all his magazines are stored. He looks down and sees himself blowing his nose into a soiled, bedraggled handkerchief right there on the cover of *Newsweek*. It is not flattering, Rizzoli admits, but he is pleased nonetheless to be on that cover.

Rizzoli decides he enjoys the attention; he's pleased to have awakened this morning to be the center of it all. *All this attention is mine,* he marvels, *without my even having left the apartment.* He is anxious to get out into the neighborhood and see how the people react to him, now that he's a celebrity.

He goes out determined not to have a big head about his newfound fame. He wants the neighborhood to know he's still a regular guy. *Same old Rizzoli. Guy never changes. That's what they'll think,* he decides.

The corner newsstand is his first stop. Inside, he stands next to the rack with the *Newsweek* magazine and waits for someone to make the connection. But no one notices that Rizzoli is the guy on the cover.

Rizzoli pulls a *Newsweek* from the rack, takes it over to Louie, and sets it down on the counter. He fumbles for change, hoping Louie will make the connection.

"You recognize this guy?" Rizzoli finally asks, pointing to the cover.

Louie studies it. "No," he says.

"It's me," Rizzoli says.

"No way."

Rizzoli smiles and confidently turns to the cover story about himself. He finds the part about his living on the Upper West Side and shows that to Louie.

"That ain't necessarily you," Louie says, after reading it. "It says the person lives on the Upper West Side, all right. Like you, okay, but it don't give no exact address. This is somebody *looks* like you." Louie tells Rizzoli a long boring story about someone he once knew who looked just like someone else he once knew.

Rizzoli makes an excuse to leave and heads for the diner, where he goes every morning for breakfast. Inside at the counter, Rizzoli orders his usual: toasted bran muffin and coffee. His friend Cheswick comes in and sits next to him.

"I'm famous," Rizzoli blurts out. *After that business with Louie, I'm not going to pussyfoot around,* he tells himself.

"Oh yeah, I have a cousin who has a friend who's famous," Cheswick says and goes on and on about his cousin's famous friend, someone Cheswick himself has

never met. "Now this friend is *really* famous," Cheswick repeats frequently. When Rizzoli persists in claiming fame for himself, Cheswick fixes him with a worried look.

"Just fooling," Rizzoli laughs.

Cheswick laughs. "Thought so. But you had me worried. Famous? You? *Come on.* But this friend of my cousin's . . ."

Finally, as Rizzoli is leaving, he feels the magazine in his pocket. He is so irritated by now that there is no way he'll show Cheswick the cover.

Rizzoli parts company with Cheswick and goes home.

For the rest of the week, Rizzoli holes up in his apartment where he watches his celebrity grow beyond all bounds. The new *Time* magazine arrives; on the cover, Rizzoli is seated for dinner at Buckingham Palace with the Queen of England and her family. Their heads are all bowed, saying grace. Rizzoli is smiling with his mouth full and there's a half-eaten roll in his hand. Rizzoli is embarrassed that millions of people will notice this. *Maybe they won't notice,* he thinks. *Of course, they'll notice.*

All that week it continues. His face is on TV constantly, his voice is on the radio endlessly. He would bore himself to death, he decides, if it weren't for the tabloids doing stories about him. He never can anticipate what they will cook up.

At the end of the week, Rizzoli heads down to Louie's and looks at *Tattler*. It shows him on the cover with a buxom blond under a headline that reads, "DOES MRS. LUNDY KNOW ABOUT RIZZOLI AND THE STRIPPER 'TEASE'?"

"There I am," Rizzoli announces, holding the tabloid up for Louie to see.

"Forget it," Louie says. "If you knew a broad like that you'd have her on your arm right now. We'd all know. How come you've never introduced her? Besides, if this was the Mrs. Lundy *we* know it wouldn't have her down as a 'beautiful, twenty-eight-year-old dame' like it says here. Mrs. Lundy's fifty, if she's a day."

Rizzoli heads for the door, miffed. On his way he notices headlines on two other tabloids. *Whisper* has "MRS. LUNDY, DO YOU KNOW WHAT THEY DID IN MARTINIQUE?" *Secret* has a photograph of Mrs. Lundy on the beach, her dress hiked up so the rolls of her nylons show on her fleshy white thighs like two doughnuts just above her knees. "WHAT DOES RIZZOLI THINK OF MRS. LUNDY'S SE-CRET LOVE LIFE?" reads the headline.

Rizzoli walks around his neighborhood. Everyone who passes him on the street has a magazine with Rizzoli on the cover: there's Rizzoli in black and white biting a loose thread on his suit jacket; Rizzoli in pink, black, and gray with some turquoise ice cream on his nose. Rizzoli sees himself passing by under other people's arms, but no one notices the *real* Rizzoli and makes the connection.

"To hell with them," Rizzoli says, and goes home. It is nine o'clock on a Saturday night. Rizzoli doesn't watch TV because the only thing on it is Rizzoli, Rizzoli, Rizzoli. Bored with Rizzoli, he goes to bed.

In his sleep, Rizzoli dreams of being a celebrity, but in the right way; where people recognize him and constantly bother him and give him no privacy at all.

"Hey, you're Rizzoli," a Puerto Rican teenager says to

him in this dream, which is set in a mom-and-pop gro-cery somewhere off in the farthest reaches of Brooklyn. "Yo! This here's Rizzoli. The famous guy. Yeah, that one there, reading the girlie magazines!"

Then Rizzoli dreams he's in a Checker cab getting ready to get out when he discovers he's left his wallet at home. He explains to the driver. The driver motions to the guy outside waiting to get into the cab. "Hey, this here's Rizzoli," the driver says. "You know, the famous guy you see on TV. He's got no money. Could you float him a five-spot for his fare?" Even with these few minor embarrassments, this dream gives Rizzoli a very great satisfaction.

RIZZOLI DREAMS ABOUT WHO IS IN THE SADDLE, HIMSELF OR THE NEW YORK TIMES Rizzoli dreams he is hurrying across 72nd Street. He is two hours late for work, but he doesn't know why. He has to rush. *I'm never this late,* he tells himself. He breaks into a run. Dodging others, Rizzoli makes his way toward the subway stop on Broadway. *Why am I this late? Why?*

A New York *Times* appears out of nowhere and nestles into Rizzoli's hand. *Like a magician's flower,* Rizzoli thinks, taking it on the run, never breaking stride. Rizzoli sees he is about a half block beyond where, on a normal morning, the *Times* always leaps into his hand. *It's running late, too,* he figures.

At the 72nd Street stop, while Rizzoli is waiting to buy his token, the *Times* jostles his arm; it's the business section wanting to get out and be read. *This* Times *wants to make up for lost time,* Rizzoli thinks. *Late newspapers must be afraid you won't get around to reading them.*

"Now wait," Rizzoli says, trying to calm down this *Times,* but it continues to jostle. "Not here. WAIT, dammit," Rizzoli finally commands. He squeezes it to his side, tightly. The *Times* stops jostling.

Rizzoli buys his token, rushes through the gate and down the stairs, taking them two at a time, when he thinks he hears the train coming. As soon as he reaches the platform, the business section flies out from under his arm, to be read.

"No. Slow down. *Slow down,* for chrissake," Rizzoli says to the section, which is already poised in mid-air.

No train yet.

Still in mid-air, the business section folds itself in half lengthwise, then folds itself in half sideways, reducing itself to the quarter size Rizzoli demands of his newspaper. The last fold is wrong, however, so it starts over, rustling, all caught up in itself.

The rustling annoys Rizzoli. He expects this *Times* to fold down noiselessly as the usual one does. But then, this is a late *Times*, he reminds himself: *A tiger of a different stripe.*

From up in mid-air, the business section drops suddenly into Rizzoli's outstretched hands. It exerts a terrific pull, causing his head to lower in a hurry. "Read. READ," this *Times* seems to be telling Rizzoli.

Rizzoli begins reading the index with summaries for the business news. It's the first thing he reads every morning on the platform; but, he reminds himself, this is not just any morning: he's late. *Where is the damn train?*

The express comes squealing in. Rizzoli jams himself into the crowded car and, in the crunch, keeps reading the business index. Rizzoli is only partway through with the top half of the column when the whole business section jerks free of Rizzoli's grasp. "Get back here," Rizzoli hollers. "I'm not finished with that."

Overhead, his business section does a frantic free-fall somersault and pitches back down into Rizzoli's hands. The bottom half of the index column stares up at him now. "Quick," it seems to say. "Quick! Quick!" Rizzoli concentrates on the index.

Rizzoli realizes Times Square is coming up just as his *Times* is overhead again, somersaulting. When it comes down, Rizzoli intends to put the business section in with the other sections, stuff the paper under his arm, and get ready to get off the train. The business section drops. Rizzoli glimpses the headline: "California Thrift Units to Merge." Instantly, the story engrosses him.

The train screeches to a stop. Rizzoli is barely able to break his attention and exit. "That's it. I've had it with you," Rizzoli says to his *Times* business section. "You just slow down. You'll get read, just hold your horses or it's the trash can for you!"

With that, the business section eases out of Rizzoli's grasp. A few feet away, in mid-air, it noiselessly unfolds itself. Slowly, methodically, it goes from quarter to full size again. Just as noiselessly and deliberately, it slides smoothly back inside the other sections held under Rizzoli's arm.

"There, there." Rizzoli is pleased he got this late *Times* to finally act like a normal *Times*. *In the morning's rush,* he thinks, *the* Times *is one thing you can count on to give you a moment's pleasure.* Rizzoli feels the paper nestling more snugly under his arm. *It is really calm now,* Rizzoli thinks as he takes off in a dead run for his office.

Why am I this late? he wonders, frantically dodging people as he runs up out of the subway and down the sidewalk to his building. *I'm never this late.* He takes the elevator to his floor and bursts in, asking the receptionist if there have been any calls for him. "No," she says, "but Mr. Whittaker has been looking for you all morning."

Rizzoli dashes to his own office, where he finds a note on his desk. He glances at the clock: 10:55. He has five minutes to get to the president's office for what the note says is "a very important matter." *Maybe he's calling me on the carpet about being late.*

Rizzoli sets his *Times* down on the desk and tears his coat off. The *Times* lies still, and Rizzoli stops to admire how patient and well-behaved it is. For an instant, it even distracts him. *It was good I talked to it,* he decides. "I'll finish reading you at lunch, don't worry," Rizzoli says, patting his *Times.* He has always finished his *Times* at lunch; somehow that gives Rizzoli confidence even in his present circumstance. "Wait here," he says to his *Times* before leaving his office.

Rizzoli scurries down the hallway, certain he is in trouble. *Now, calm down,* Rizzoli tells himself. As Rizzoli approaches the president's office, the secretary motions him in. He enters and finds the president in a solemn mood.

They exchange quick pleasantries, but to Rizzoli their conversation seems stilted.

It's me, Rizzoli thinks.

Mr. Whittaker explains to Rizzoli that a competitor has been stealing trade secrets and their company is going to file suit.

Rizzoli is greatly relieved. *Mr. Whittaker's being on edge really has nothing to do with me personally,* he thinks.

Mr. Whittaker says that he needs Rizzoli's advice. Then he explains the possible strategies. "Which one do you think we ought to go with?" Mr. Whittaker asks, "Let me hear your thinking."

The secretary comes in and asks to speak to Mr. Whittaker outside.

"Mull this over and let me know what you think when I return," Mr. Whittaker says as he leaves.

"Will do," Rizzoli says.

Sitting and waiting, Rizzoli thinks hard about the strategies. Suddenly, the business section of the *Times* comes up behind him noiselessly and hovers over his head. Rizzoli is still weighing the various strategies and doesn't notice. At 12:15, the business section plummets down into Rizzoli's hands.

Not here! NOT NOW! Rizzoli thinks as he clasps the paper. He struggles to resist, but the business section lowers his head. It exerts great force. *It knows it is 12:15 and I should be in the restaurant reading it, but what can I do?* The business section trembles expectantly in his hands. "Read. *Now.* Read," the *Times* seems to be telling Rizzoli. *It's terrified I won't have the time to read it.*

"Now calm down. It'll be all right," Rizzoli says soothingly, but the *Times* soon has Rizzoli bent over reading about California thrifts, right where he'd left off earlier.

Mr. Whittaker returns to find Rizzoli reading the *Times*. "Well," he says coolly.

Rizzoli does not look up. This *Times* won't let him go now. It has him deeply engrossed, and he goes on reading.

Mr. Whittaker clears his throat to get Rizzoli's attention. "WELL?"

Rizzoli goes on reading about the California thrifts.

"PUT THAT PAPER DOWN!"

Rizzoli manages a little nod, but he can't stop reading.

Mr. Whittaker angrily tells him to get out, but Rizzoli sits in the president's office a while longer to finish the story on the thrifts, before he switches to another business story. "Price Plotting on Tubing is Charged." He goes out, still reading.

Back in his own office, Rizzoli puts on his coat without interrupting his reading. The business section won't let him look up. The other sections of the *Times* collect themselves, fly off his desk, and slide under his arm. These sections shake impatiently to be read.

"YOU'LL GET READ," Rizzoli screams, "I promise. If business just lets me loose."

"LET ME LOOSE!"

The business section tightens its grip. It has Rizzoli reading faster and faster. "Read! READ!" Rizzoli seems to hear. "It's *this* late," the sections under his arm seem to chorus, "and you're still on *business*? How do you expect to get to us? HOW? HOW?" The business section keeps Rizzoli glued to its pages. "READ!" Rizzoli goes out and down the hallway, reading. He passes the receptionist, still reading.

"Mr. Rizzoli, could I have the keys to your office?" the receptionist asks, "You have been dismissed."

"Uh-huh, uh-huh," Rizzoli says absentmindedly, giving her the keys and wondering all the while, *Why am I still on business?*

Walking out, Rizzoli gets on the elevator, still reading business. He goes down the street and heads for his restaurant, still reading business.

A half block down the street, Rizzoli still has his head down reading when suddenly the business section leaves his hand. Listlessly, it floats a few feet away, then wafts ever so slowly down into a wire mesh trash can. Business has quit.

Rizzoli is dismayed at the sight of a New York *Times* quitting. "It's only ten minutes to one. Don't quit. WINNERS NEVER QUIT, Rizzoli hollers at it lying down there

on top of discarded French fries smeared with catsup.
"QUITTERS NEVER WIN!"

Now the other sections slide out from under Rizzoli's arm and waft down on top of business.

"CHICKEN!"

"GUTLESS WONDER!"

"YELLOW BELLY!"

When Rizzoli stops shouting at the *Times* he suddenly feels an odd sense of relief. He has not felt this relaxed since yesterday, when Mr. Whittaker indicated he might include Rizzoli on the new project. *Before this* Times *descended on me.*

Rizzoli gets the impulse to reach down and rub the *Times* in the catsup. He looks down but sees it is just an old newspaper now. Lifeless.

RIZZOLI DREAMS OF BEING UNEMPLOYED Rizzoli dreams he is dressed and sitting at the kitchen table having his cold cereal and milk. He glances at the clock: *One-thirty in the afternoon,* he thinks. *I should be at work.* Then he remembers that he is unemployed.

Rizzoli goes over in his mind once again how he was let go from his job. *HOW is all I know,* he thinks. *I still don't know WHY.* Once again, in his mind, Rizzoli sees himself standing in front of Mr. Whittaker's desk. "We just don't need you anymore, Rizzoli," Mr. Whittaker says. "It's nothing personal, you understand that. I like you, but . . ."

"I understand," Rizzoli remembers saying in a pleasant way. Smiling. The good soldier.

Why didn't I stand up for myself? Rizzoli remembers he even asked Mr. Whittaker, "Would it be more convenient for you, Mr. Whittaker, if I left on Wednesday or Friday?"

"Thank you for asking," Mr. Whittaker answered, "but right now is fine."

"Is there any reason for your letting me go?" Rizzoli remembers asking at this point. "Any particular reason?"

"No reason," Mr. Whittaker answered. "We just don't need you anymore, you understand. Nothing personal."

"I understand. Thank you," Rizzoli said, trying to remember how long he'd been with the company. *Years and years.*

Rizzoli erases the scene from his mind and goes out and down the stairs. He checks his mailbox. There is one envelope. Rizzoli opens it and reads the form letter:

Dear Occupant,

This letter is to notify you of the general well-being of the sender. May your day be pleasant and your health good.

Best regards,

It is signed "Mother." He looks at the envelope; the return address says "Mrs. E. P. Rizzoli." He puts himself in his mother's place, and he can understand. *Her son is out of work; this is her first letter after she knows. What else can you expect?*

Rizzoli goes out of his building and walks toward Columbus Avenue. A guy bumps into him. "Sorry, I didn't see you there," the guy says. A little further on another guy bumps into him and says, "Watch where you're going."

On the corner, Rizzoli sees his friend Cheswick.

"Cheswick," Rizzoli says.

Cheswick looks around, puzzled. He stares blankly at Rizzoli.

"Right here, Cheswick," Rizzoli says. "Here! HERE!"

Cheswick still shows no sign of recognition. "Right in front of you, Cheswick." Cheswick turns away and looks down Columbus. Rizzoli does too, and he sees their mutual friend, Byron, approaching.

What are these two doing wandering around? Rizzoli suddenly thinks. *Shouldn't they be working?* Then he remembers: *It's Saturday.*

"Cheswick," says Byron. "Just the man I want to see. Elizabeth and I are having a few friends for dinner tonight. We wondered if you could make it on the spur of the moment?"

"Sure," says Cheswick. "That'd be fine."

"Eight o'clock," Byron says. "and bring . . ." Byron nods faintly toward Rizzoli. "If you want to," he adds.

Rizzoli is disappointed; he has the strange feeling that both Byron and Cheswick are very angry at him. But he doesn't know why. He dismisses it. *Maybe it's my problem,* he thinks. *Sure, it must be.*

Rizzoli goes back to his building and checks his mail again. *Might have missed something,* he thinks. He has. He opens the small envelope and reads:

To Whom It May Concern:

It is our pleasure to invite you to attend a dinner tonight. It will be served from 8:30–9:30. It will be casual.

With pleasure, your hosts,
Byron and Elizabeth Bayley

That night Rizzoli dresses and goes to the Bayleys' co-op on the Upper West Side. The doorman directs him to the elevator. Rizzoli goes up to the fourteenth floor and down the hallway. In front of the Bayley's door, 14E, Rizzoli stands and rings the bell for a long while.

Finally the door opens. "Well, well, if it isn't Cheswick," says Elizabeth. "Come in." Cheswick and his date, Angie, enter behind Rizzoli who realizes that they had evidently been standing behind him, silently, for some time.

Everyone sits down in the Bayleys' living room.

Rizzoli is offered a seat behind the Boston fern. Everyone talks for a while. Rizzoli doesn't speak up; he doesn't want to draw attention to himself. *People will start asking me questions if I do. "You were fired, weren't you?" "Do you think you'll ever get another job?"*

"Dinner is served," Elizabeth says. "Please come. Byron will seat you."

Rizzoli goes to the table and finds there is no place set for him. *There would be if I had a job.* Without looking at him, the hostess passes Rizzoli a note, which reads:

To Whom It May Concern,

For your pleasure and eating enjoyment, your hosts have set a place for you in the newly redecorated kitchen.

Your Hosts
Byron and Elizabeth Bayley

In the kitchen Rizzoli finds a place set for him. His plate is a plastic container divided into equal sections containing perfect round scoops of potato salad and quiche. Rizzoli has never seen quiche served in a scoop like ice cream, but there it is. A sheet of plastic wrap covers his food. In cellophane wrappers by the side of his plate, he finds white plastic utensils, a packet of sugar and smaller packets of salt and pepper.

Rizzoli eats. Muzak plays in the background; Rizzoli recognizes the theme song from "Chariots of Fire"; he can hear the other guests out in the dining room laughing and talking.

Occasionally, overhearing the others, Rizzoli silently adds something to their conversation. He thinks of being fired and how great his life used to be before that. Now, in the exact same way he used to laugh out loud back then, he mimes a silent laugh.

But suddenly his vision blurs and his forehead flashes burning hot. His first thought is dread that he may pass out in Elizabeth's kitchen. *GOD FORBID! Oh, here's the hostess now.* Rizzoli smiles, even though his vision is a bad blur.

Elizabeth ignores Rizzoli and keeps up a conversation with the guests in the other room as she slices more turkey onto a serving plate and gets more dressing.

Rizzoli needs an aspirin desperately but doesn't want to bother her when she's so busy. His head is ablaze but still he thinks. *It wouldn't be fair to make her go out of her way on my behalf—when she's busy with the dressing.* The hostess turns and goes away with the platters. Too late anyway. Rizzoli is in dreadful pain now.

Soon Elizabeth, Angie, and the other women are clearing the dishes. They bring them into the kitchen and start stacking them on the kitchen table. With the women buzzing around him, Rizzoli hopes all the more for an easing of this headache. His pain increases instead. As the women clatter plates all around him, his head splits, and he feels irritation at their lack of consideration. But he can't blame them, he thinks, because they don't know he has a headache. *And they're SURELY not to blame for my firing.*

For an instant his irritation swells into a powerful anger at these women, and as it does, his headache eases and his symptoms subside somewhat. But he hardly notices; he is too alarmed that the anger he feels seems so powerful it might erupt. He denies it instantly. *I'm a guest. I can't show anger.* He fights back this anger which almost overwhelms him before it subsides.

Then the loud hubbub eases as the women get a chocolate cake and plates and bring these into the dining room. On her way out, Elizabeth hands Rizzoli a note:

To Whom It May Concern,

If you should desire dessert, please turn this card over.

Rizzoli turns it over.

For your pleasure and eating enjoyment, there is one serving of ready-made custard in a plastic container in the refrigerator.

Your Hosts,
Byron and Elizabeth Bayley

Rizzoli is full and decides to pass on the dessert. He is sure the headache will be back to get him, but for now he is feeling all right. He listens to Muzak for a while. He falls asleep.

He wakes up to hear the party ending. Elizabeth comes into the kitchen bringing some glasses. She sets them down, hands Rizzoli a note and goes into the other room.

Dear Guest,

It has been our pleasure to serve you.
Come again.

Your Hosts
Byron and Elizabeth Bayley

Rizzoli goes into the bedroom. His coat is the last one left on the bed. He puts it on and joins the others, who are saying good-bye at the door.

Byron and Elizabeth say good-bye to everyone passing out the door.

"I had a great time," Rizzoli says. "Thank you."

"You're welcome," Byron and Elizabeth say to Cheswick and Angie.

Byron and Elizabeth wave and close their door.

The elevator arrives and he crowds on with everyone else. It starts down. Rizzoli stands staring straight at the doors with everyone at his back talking about what a fine dinner party it was.

Rizzoli feels himself gliding down smoothly when suddenly the elevator jerks spasmodically and stops. The doors don't open. "What?" those behind him exclaim in startled voices. "Are we between floors?" one asks. They start frantically pressing the different floor buttons, but to no avail. One of them says, "We must be stuck."

Rizzoli doesn't say anything; he wants to remain as inconspicuous as possible. But he feels his headache coming back. He dreads what he might do right there in the stalled elevator. Then he hears them whispering behind his back. Anger wells up inside him. It's so powerful he knows he won't be able to fight it back. He fears it's taking on a life of its own.

Although he resists, the anger whirls him around to face the other Bayley partygoers, who immediately glance downward, unable to look Rizzoli in the eyes. Rizzoli is embarrassed for them. He feels himself fix everyone with an icy stare, even as he thinks, *Can't they see it's the anger doing this? Not me?*

"So, life is unfair you say?" Rizzoli suddenly asks them with a voice so seething in anger that he doesn't recognize it as his own. "UNFAIR FOR *ME* ONLY, YOU THINK, AND NEVER FOR ANY OF YOU, RIGHT? YOU? YOU?" Rizzoli's finger is stabbing at each of them. He tries to stop it but can't. "YOU? YOU? YOU? YOU?" his voice screams accusingly.

They don't answer Rizzoli who now realizes with terror that he's helpless to stop his own raging voice. He tries to say something different. *I CAN'T.* He closes his lips, but his voice rages on uncontrollably inside the elevator.

Rizzoli is mortified at the shame he is causing them. *If they'd only look up and see my lips are closed, they'd know I'm a prisoner of this raging voice. Can't they see?* "WELL, YOU'D BETTER THINK AGAIN!" his voice rages on.

Struggling to calm the voice, he tries in quick succession, a smile, an "Oh, Shucks" gesture, a slight bemused look. Anything. It does no good.

How to control IT? he wonders. He tries to get his lips in sync with what the rage is saying. It works: his mind suddenly moves his lips to shout, right along, "LOOK UP AT ME AND SAY YOU WON'T EVER NOT SEE ME AGAIN!" He brings his hand up and quickly stabs the air, as he remembers doing involuntarily earlier at each one. "YOU. YOU. YOU. YOU. YOU. YOU."

Each one glances up, looks him in the face and says, in a meek voice, "I'll never not see you again, Rizzoli."

The elevator starts moving again.

RIZZOLI DREAMS OF GETTING A LETTER FROM AN OLD FRIEND

March 6
Dear Rizzoli,

This is just a short note to let you know that last week I lost all motor function and will not be able to come to New York City next month for our annual get-together. I know I told you in an earlier letter about my illness so I won't go into detail here.

Rizzoli stops reading. He is shocked. There was no earlier letter and Rizzoli had no previous knowledge of his friend's illness. He reads on:

I also thought you'd like to know Dooley is dead of cancer. I hope all is well with you.

Your friend,

Pete
P.S. Agnes wrote this.

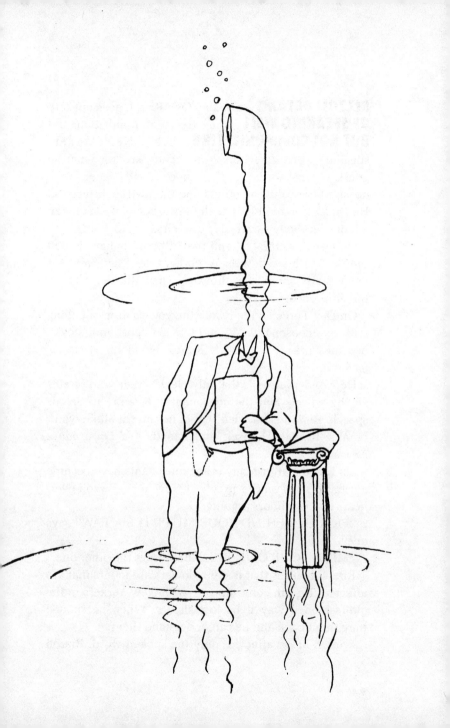

RIZZOLI DREAMS On Day One Rizzoli goes out into **OF SPEAKING WELL** the streets of Manhattan and **BUT NOT COMMUNICATING** hears New Yorkers speaking words like "slp," "mt," and "kp" for what he guesses must be "sleep," "meet," and "keep." He doesn't know. But the others don't know the difference. He finds it incredible that the lowercase "e" has fallen out of everybody's everyday discourse.

On Day Two the "a" and the "u" vowels have joined the "e," so his fellow New Yorkers now say "np" for "nap" and "sbwy" for subway." They still don't know the difference.

On Day Three all the rest of the vowels drop out along with two consonants "l" and "n." So "pork loin steak" becomes prk   stk." Rizzoli wonders, *What the fuck is it?*

He wonders if he is the only New Yorker who retains all the vowels and the consonants "l" and "n" in his speech. Rizzoli is terrified that in no time at all he won't be able to make himself understood. *And I'm a native New Yorker.*

On Day Six after many other consonants have become ancient history on the streets of New York, Rizzoli over-hears two neighbors arguing:

"PICK UP BEHIND YOUR MUTT. IT'S A LAW," says one.

"MIND YOUR OWN BUSINESS," says the other one.

Rizzoli realizes that it's only lower-case letters that are affected. He can communicate with New Yorkers in the old-fashioned way if he just shouts. When he shouts, they shout back and he can understand them.

Print is never affected, only the spoken word. Rizzoli

reads in the *Times* on Day Nine that it is "a virus communicated to humans over the telephone network of New York and southern Connecticut." His touch dial phone has been out of order, so Rizzoli is spared.

Overall, he doesn't mind; it's not too much different from the way it always was. But he does wonder how the *Times* reporters get their stories. *By shouting?*

RIZZOLI'S DREAM
OF SILENCE
AND HUMILIATION
Rizzoli dreams he is passing
time in the lobby of Lincoln Center before the opera. Rizzoli loves just
looking at the people—at the women in mink, the men
in their tuxedos.

Rizzoli himself has rented a tuxedo for the occasion.
As he stands gazing at the crowd, he tries to affect the
same bemused indifference he sees reflected on the
faces of other people in the crowd. Though this is his
first time at the opera, Rizzoli feels he has the look
down. *Who's to know I'm not a regular season ticket
holder?* he thinks.

Suddenly he has the uneasy feeling that someone is
close behind him. He turns around to see. *Not him*, he
thinks. *Not here.*

The mime who shows up periodically in Rizzoli's life
to humiliate him is now standing there gazing back at
Rizzoli in the exact same way Rizzoli is gazing at him.
Squinting his eyes in anger, Rizzoli mutters, "Beat it,"" in
a discreet tone. The mime squints back at Rizzoli. Then
the mime's expression turns blank: black star-crossed
eyes stare out from the chalk white face.

Rizzoli looks him straight in the eye and glares, getting
no reaction. He decides to ignore him and turns his back
to the mime.

Rizzoli puts his hand to his chin and tries to look nonchalant. He hears a wave of giggles. Rizzoli glances
down at the floor, trying to ignore all the people smiling
and staring his way. He is getting angry but tries not to
show it. He folds his hands across his chest. He hears
movement in back of him. Another wave of giggles.

"That's it, son-of-a-bitch," Rizzoli screams and turns

on the mime. "I've had it with you!"

Rizzoli begins punching. Lefts. Rights.

The mime always evades the blows and winds up directly behind Rizzoli, punching in rhythm with him. Lefts. Rights.

It's nearly curtain time. The crowd thins out. Rizzoli continues fighting the mime. Soon they are the only ones left in the lobby.

An usher comes out and walks past. The mime turns, follows the usher—imitating his walk—and disappears.

Rizzoli is greatly relieved. He ducks into the darkened opera house where an usher stops him. "Sorry," he says. "No seating fifteen minutes after the performance has begun." Rizzoli has to leave.

————

In the men's room of the Roosevelt Hotel in midtown, Rizzoli is washing his hands. The gray-haired attendant comes over and hands Rizzoli a white towel.

"Thanks," Rizzoli says, setting the towel down. *Am I supposed to tip him now?* he wonders. *Or do I leave a tip in here?* The plate is on the wash basin. Rizzoli looks at it. *But that's the soap dish, isn't it?* The attendant keeps standing there, smiling. Rizzoli doesn't know how much to give him. He hesitates. The attendant turns his back to Rizzoli and walks away.

At this instant Rizzoli looks in the mirror and thinks he sees the mime standing behind him. Shrugging his shoulders, the mime exaggerates a flustered look.

"Get out of here!" Rizzoli screams at the mime.

"Sir, I belong here," the attendant says.

"I don't mean you," Rizzoli says. The attendant looks puzzled. Rizzoli and the attendant are the only ones in the men's room.

"Sorry," Rizzoli says, embarrassed. He walks over to the attendant and hands him a five-dollar bill.

Rizzoli is with Mrs. Lundy in a gallery at the Metropolitan Museum. They are looking at abstract paintings in the show "A Retrospective of Modernism." Mrs. Lundy has the impression that Rizzoli is an art expert, and Rizzoli does not try to dissuade her from this opinion. The day before, Rizzoli came to the show and memorized the names of some painters and their work.

Now, from a distance, Rizzoli points to a big abstract with slashing strokes of black on a white background and tells Mrs. Lundy it's a Franz Kline. "'Untitled No. 8,' I think," Rizzoli adds. Mrs. Lundy, who doesn't know one abstract painter from another, nods in agreement.

"Oh, I like this," Mrs. Lundy says, pointing to the next painting. "That stripe of red is the same exact color as the wallpaper I chose for my hallway."

Rizzoli turns and sees the mime. The mime points at the painting with a look of certainty that exaggerates the expression on Mrs. Lundy's face.

It's one thing to mock me, Rizzoli thinks. *But Mrs. Lundy?*

Rizzoli walks toward the mime. The mime turns his back and walks away; his walk is a perfect imitation of Rizzoli's.

Rizzoli runs after him. Then the mime is running after

Rizzoli running after the mime. His imitation of Rizzoli running is perfect.

Rizzoli stops. He falls to his knees and starts pounding the floor in frustration.

Five feet away from him, the mime is doing the same thing.

Rizzoli is bent over like this when he hears Mrs. Lundy say, "No, Rizzoli, you're wrong." She is standing by the first painting Rizzoli pointed out to her. "This one isn't by that Franz Kline. It says here it's by this Robert Motherwell. You were right, though; it is 'Untitled.' But not No. 8. It's No. 415."

"Four hundred and *fifteen*?" Rizzoli asks, turning around to look at Mrs. Lundy. When he turns back, the mime has disappeared.

THE DREAM OF RIZZOLI Rizzoli reads the *Times* on
LOST IN ILLUSION the uptown local subway going to
BLIND TO REALITY 72nd Street.

He lowers his paper. He observes the young woman sitting across from him. He imagines her naked. He imagines slowly undressing her, taking off one item of her clothing at a time, as she sits attractively and stylishly dressed, staring past him.

He raises his paper up again and continues reading from where he left off.

With his paper totally blocking his view of her, the young woman now sits completely naked. Her body is very different from what Rizzoli imagined. Other riders on the subway see her naked but pay no attention. Rizzoli lowers his paper.

She is dressed.

He raises his paper.

She is naked.

He lowers his paper.

She is dressed.

He raises his paper.

She is naked.

She is naked as she exits her stop. Rizzoli doesn't notice as he continues reading his *Times*.

THE DREAM OF RIZZOLI Rizzoli dreams he's in his
LEARNING STARTLING FACTS big chair in the living
ABOUT A FEW GUYS room idly watching TV.
IN THE NEIGHBORHOOD "Coming up next," says
the voice-over, "a surprising look at some of your
neighbors."

Rizzoli isn't particularly interested, but there's nothing good on the other channels so he keeps the program on while he reads the paper.

"Now, we know everyone wants to learn secrets about other people's lives. So in the next hour, we are going to introduce you to five New Yorkers—average people like yourself—and we are going to let you in on some startling never-before-revealed facts about their personal histories. The people you will see are all your neighbors on the Upper West Side, but they might as well be anyone's neighbors anywhere in New York City, out there in America, or any place in the world."

Now the host comes on himself, saying: "Hello. I'm Bert Simmons, your host for tonight. I'd like to welcome you to 'Startling News.' First up on our show tonight we'd like you to meet a man who owns the corner newsstand at 75th and Columbus." He introduces Louie.

Louie? Rizzoli looks up. *LOUIE?* He puts the newspaper down and watches.

Bert Simmons and Louie are talking. Louie is telling Bert about the problems he's having with late deliveries of the New York *Times* and they discuss the magazines that are really moving lately. "But it's Lotto that really makes a newsstand go nowadays," Louie says.

"A fact we all appreciate," Bert says, turning to the camera to wink. Then he turns back to Louie. "Louie?"

he says, "you say you have personally killed fifteen hundred human beings."

Fifteen hundred? Rizzoli thinks. *A mass murderer? Louie? No.*

"Right," says Louie.

Rizzoli almost falls off his couch. *No.*

Bert is explaining that Louie was a fighter pilot in the Pacific during World War II. Rizzoli is relieved. *That's war. That's different.*

"By my own careful estimate," Louie's saying, "I figure I killed about fifteen hundred Japanese." The camera comes in to focus on Louie using his pocket calculator. He's explaining the statistical formula he devised and uses to do the figuring. Bert says, "But even with a formula like Louie's, and even using a calculator, human error is bound to enter in." Bert smiles. "So to check the totals, we've gone to our own computer. And, Louie, here's some 'Startling News' for you: the correct figure for the total number of humans killed by you in World War II is 8,412!"

Eight thousand four hundred and twelve?

"That many, huh?" Louie asks. "You sure?" He is punching numbers into the pocket calculator as if he's trying to see where his statistical formula went wrong.

Bert winks at the camera. "The computer," he says, "is never wrong."

"Right," says Louie. "No sense arguing with that."

Louie was smart there, Rizzoli thinks. *You can't argue with one of those computers.*

Bert is going on about how Louie's total breaks down with only about seventy-five percent of the humans being Japanese. The other quarter were Pacific Island natives, who were, Bert adds, non-combatants.

Next up, Bert introduces Eddie. Rizzoli immediately recognizes Eddie as the owner of the Japanese restaurant up the block from Louie's newsstand. Bert and Eddie chat. Eddie tells Bert he came to the U.S. in 1958. He loves the Upper West Side and all the exciting things that are happening in the neighborhood. He says business is good and getting better, and Bert says that that's because the food's so good.

Rizzoli nods. He loves the *donburi* at Eddie's.

But now Bert is telling Eddie's story. Eddie was a fighter pilot during World War II but on the other side. "I killed, I don't know, maybe two thousand, with bombing, with strafing." He lifts his shoulders a little. "No more than that. Maybe less."

"That's your estimate?" Bert asks, and when Eddie nods, Bert says, "then let's go now to the computer! Which gives us the total number of humans killed by Eddie as—*9,122!*"

Eddie frowns and shakes his head a little. "I used a calculator too. Maybe I got it wrong because I used the same statistical formula as Louie?"

Eddie? Rizzoli thinks, remembering the *donburi. Nine thousand dead?*

Eddie's head is down and he isn't really listening. Bert is breaking down the total: only two-thirds were American, he's saying, with the other third being those Pacific Islanders.

Now Eddie's gone off, and Bert is introducing a distinguished looking older gentleman, a regular in the breakfast crowd at the local coffee shop. Rizzoli doesn't know him to speak to, but he learns now his name is Karl.

He's sixty years old, he's saying, in a German accent. He was born and raised in Bavaria. He came to the U.S. in 1952.

"I was with the forces on the Western Front," Karl says, "but I was badly wounded—I still limp with it—so I was taken out of action almost immediately. So, to the best of my knowledge, I can tell you I killed nobody." He pushes his bottom lip out.

Bert winks. The lights on the computer blink and flash, and it begins to print out. Bert reads with good humor: "Karl wasn't an infantryman, it seems, but a bomber pilot with the Luftwaffe. Karl you're too modest. It says here you killed eighty thousand humans."

Did he say eighty thousand? Rizzoli asks. *One guy? In my neighborhood?*

Bert is giving the breakdown: "Twenty-four thousand British, including civilians, 11,014 Belgians, all civilians, 9,214 Americans, all military personnel . . ."

"This is not so!" Karl shouts. "That computer LIES! I was badly wounded! I still limp with it! I was taken out of the action immediately!"

Bert seems a little taken aback at being interrupted, but is still in good humor. "The computer has never been wrong to date," he says. "But you're free to check the printout for errors, Karl." A man comes onto the set with a wheelbarrow heaped with mounds of computer printouts. "They're all here," Bert says. "The deaths. Their names are listed in alphabetical order, then age, sex, nationality. You can check them if you want to, one by one."

A wheelbarrow?

Bert's on to the next guest, another guy from the coffee shop. This one's Russian, named Nick. Nick was a Russian sailor who jumped ship in 1962 and was given political asylum.

"Ya," Nick's saying, "I killed plenty of Germans during the war. Altogether, I killed maybe thirty-nine thousand, if you count Kulaks."

"Yes, Nick," Bert says as he winks at the audience. "Kulaks count." He goes on to explain that Kulaks were the Russian farmers who resisted collectivization during the 1930s. Approximately twenty million Kulaks were killed, Bert mentions.

By Nick? No!

"Nick," Bert is saying, "the computer gives your total as fifty-one thousand! Twenty-three thousand Russians, and the 12,104 Poles . . ."

"No Poles," Nick says. "I'm Russian. I killed Germans. A few Kulaks, maybe, but no Poles."

". . . 12,104 Poles," Bert continues, "when the Soviet Union was still allied with Germany during 1940?"

"Oh, that," Nick says. "I forgot about that."

"*Then*, there were the 16,248 Germans *after* Germany attacked Russia."

"Right," Nick says. "It was the Poles I forgot."

"And you didn't know if you had to count Kulaks," Bert says.

Next is Mark, the guy who owns the tennis shop. He always says hello as Rizzoli passes by. He's in his mid-thirties, Rizzoli learns, and was a B-52 bomber pilot in Vietnam.

"I really don't have a very good idea of how many I killed," Mark's saying. "Twenty thousand, maybe, but it could be more, a lot more." He explains that he was flying at such high altitudes that there was no way of seeing where the bombs were falling. "A lot of them were dumped into free-fire zones, where anything alive had been classified as being 'enemy.'" Mark says.

"Well, let's not keep you in the dark about your totals." Bert says. "For your two hundred and twelve bombing missions over Vietnam, you got 17,814 Vietnamese, with the breakdown there going like this: Eleven percent North Vietnamese regular troops, twenty-three percent South Vietnamese regular troops, and the other sixty-six percent a mix of guerrillas and noncombatants—even the computer has a little trouble with that one, you know, telling the difference. There were also the two hundred and eighteen American soldiers killed on the ground by friendly fire."

"Sorry about those two hundred and eighteen," Mark says.

"Aren't we all?" Bert asks, conversationally. Already he's booming out Mark's totals.

Eighteen thousand. Eighteen thousand dead, did he say? A guy my own age? The guy from the tennis shop?

"You know," Mark's saying, "in a funny way I'm kinda relieved. I know it sounds bad, but I was sorta thinking it might have been a lot higher than that, double that, maybe. I mean eighteen thousand is bad enough, but I'm just glad it isn't a hundred thousand."

Glad it's not a hundred thousand? Rizzoli thinks. *Me too.* He can't remember the last time he's watched a program so intently. He's sitting on the edge of the couch, watching as Mark shakes hands with Bert and leaves.

"And now," Bert says, "we're ready for the totals. The five guests on our show tonight—Louie, Eddie, Karl, Nick, and Mark—have killed a total of . . ." A woman comes on stage and hands Bert a slip of paper. ". . . one hundred sixty thousand!" Bert goes into the breakdown: Six thousand five hundred Japanese, seventeen thousand Americans, twenty-three thousand Russians, sixteen thousand Germans, rounded off. Three, make that four thousand Pacific Islanders."

Rizzoli is losing track. *Five guys?* he thinks. *Five guys from the neighborhood?* But then he remembers: *It was war.*

Bert is still talking, going, ". . . and just so you don't think we've singled out one neighborhood unfairly we'll switch you to another part of the city." The camera pans a street scene and moves in to show a crowded sidewalk with two, streams of pedestrians, one coming toward the camera with Bert's voice-over saying: "Here's a typical scene in midtown Manhattan." A white arrow on the screen points out an old man. "This man, for instance, is nearly eighty and has killed a total of one hundred and eight humans in his lifetime, according to our computer."

Rizzoli suddenly sees himself come into view, walking along in the crowd. *That's me!*

Now the white arrow moves over to point at the man moving along elbow to elbow with Rizzoli, immediately to his right.

"This man is thirty-three, and we're informed he has killed one human, quite recently in fact."

Rizzoli brings his hands to his mouth and starts to chew his fingernails.

Now the arrow is pointing to a man on Rizzoli's left. He's killed 3,812 humans. Now it moves to the guy ten feet behind Rizzoli, who has killed six.

"So what we've learned," Bert says, "is simply this: you don't want to find yourself on the wrong side of the fence from people like Louie, Eddie, Karl, Nick and Mark. So from all of us here at 'Startling News,' I'm Bert Simmons and I'd like to wish you a very pleasant evening."

Now the theme music comes on and a printed message appears on the TV screen. Rizzoli dreams he reads:

The computer information used in this program is available upon request under the Freedom of Information Act. If you want to inquire about how many humans you have killed in your lifetime, or to find out if you have killed anyone at all, write:

Department of Casualties
Bureau of Statistics
P.O. Box 9872
Washington, D.C. 80024

RIZZOLI DREAMS OF THE ULTIMATE COMPLAINT OF NEW YORKERS "New Yorkers will complain. New Yorkers wouldn't be New Yorkers if they couldn't complain. I personally couldn't stand it if we DIDN'T complain."

It's Mayor Jimmy the Whack holding forth on some local round table talk show that Rizzoli has just tuned into on his Walkman, while riding the subway back to Manhattan from Kennedy Airport. He has just returned from a business trip, and, for a change, decided to take the well-advertised subway service back to the city.

". . . in the end I personally have found New Yorkers respect a Mayor like myself who is WORTH COMPLAINING ABOUT. New Yorkers discriminate, they don't complain about just ANYBODY. A city official has to DESERVE THEIR COMPLAINTS. New Yorkers are great, great, great— they're special."

Shut up, you half-wit. Rizzoli is very suspicious now; the Mayor's words have put Rizzoli on guard. *Every time he's ever given the "New Yorkers Will Complain" speech,* Rizzoli notes, *he's put something BIG over on us. What is it now? How bad could it be?* Rizzoli wonders. *I've only been away three weeks. How badly could the Mayor screw us in that little time?*

". . . and one reason they're special is they DO COM-PLAIN. They have the COURAGE TO COMPLAIN. (A long pause) I have the good sense to make them complain and they love me for giving them the chance to do what THEY DO BEST.

"AND I praise the great, great people of New York City for

realizing, after all their complaining is said and done, that this great, great city needs more and more revenue . . ."

Now HALF WIT is finally getting to the point, Rizzoli thinks.

"As your humble servant," the Mayor continues, "I am merely following the lead of all New Yorkers everywhere in demanding more revenue for the great needs of this great, great city."

Sudden screeching signals the subway is coming to its terminus in Manhattan, and after a jarring stop Rizzoli grabs his single suitcase and joins the others in exiting the air-conditioned car, into a wall of hot, humid air. It's a scorching August day, and down in the subway tunnel it must be in the nineties. Rizzoli heads for the IRT line uptown.

As he does, he keeps listening to his Walkman and hears the Mayor's Commissioner of Frustration, Leffkowitz, saying to the round table host, "Six years ago I said, 'Your Honor, the average New Yorker's frustration level is now so low that unless you do something to raise it you're never going to get re-elected. *Frustrate* them,' I said, 'and you instantly draw attention to yourself as Mayor.' His Honor said to me then, 'Brilliant. That's it, Leffkowitz.' "

Sweating heavily as he lugs his suitcase, Rizzoli grows impatient to know. *What is it exactly? What specifically are they talking about?* Rizzoli still doesn't know as he gets on the Number 1 Local uptown to 72nd Street. It's another air-conditioned car, and Rizzoli's sweating body instantly turns cold and clammy.

Rizzoli keeps listening to his Walkman. As the subway pulls into the 66th Street stop, he finally gets a little clue as to what is being discussed when the round table host says to the Mayor's Commissioner of Hostility, Amerigo O'Dilly. "But pedestrians are voters too. Aren't you and the Mayor forgetting that, Mr. O'Dilly?"

Pedestrians? Rizzoli thinks, aghast. *He screwed poor helpless pedestrians? How? What is it specifically? Maybe O'Dilly will say . . .*

"The Mayor is not forgetting anything," the Commissioner of Hostility says. "His Honor knows you have to incite mass hostility before you can channel it in a positive direction. ALL the more power to whomever can BOTH CAUSE and then CHANNEL popular hostility in a direction beneficial to ALL."

The Mayor interrupts at this point by saying, "New Yorkers are great, great and their hostility is another reason for their greatness."

Whatever the Mayor has done to New Yorkers, Rizzoli knows now that it's bad, REAL BAD. His apprehension grows as his train comes to a stop at 72nd, and he exits into the incredible heat of the underground subway platform. He doesn't know what to expect as he starts up the stairs. On leaving this subway station, Rizzoli knows he'll have to go another four blocks (*as a PEDES-TRIAN!*) to get to his apartment on 75th. Sweating again before he's even up the stairs, Rizzoli takes off his Walkman and readies himself for the worst the Mayor could do to New Yorkers.

"Holy Mother of God!" he exclaims as he exits onto 72nd Street; he can't believe it. *Who am I? How long was I gone on my business trip? Five years? Ten? Twenty? When did HE do all this? Was I sleeping for years out of town while the Mayor DIDDLED US?*

THE CROWDS. HERE ON ALL THE STREETS' SIDEWALKS. HUGE CROWDS, Rizzoli thinks. Everywhere he looks he sees people jammed on sidewalks on all the streets as far as his eye can see. *No wonder,* he suddenly notes, *what kind of sidewalks are THESE?* His eye has caught something new and ominous: the streets sidewalks are penned in at the curb with cyclone fences so the dense crowds inch along, jammed between the buildings and this fence. *What the BE-JEEZUS?* Rizzoli asks the guy next to him about the strange fenced sidewalks.

"Toll sidewalks," this New Yorker explains nonchalantly, as if he'd seen and accepted everything.

"Toll sidewalks?" Rizzoli asks. *TOLL SIDEWALKS?* Rizzoli thinks. He can't believe it. *Is this incredible, or what? HALF WIT really humped the city on this one.*

"Toll sidewalks," the guy repeats. "You pay or you can't get where you're going. Where you going? You must be a tourist."

Rizzoli doesn't know how to answer that. *TOURIST? Here I am a native New Yorker and schmo here asks that? How long have I been gone?* Rizzoli debates asking how the toll sidewalks work but when he finally decides to swallow his pride and sound like a tourist asking, he glances up and finds the guy has disappeared. *Guy could care less about any tourist—that's New York.*

Rizzoli moves towards the nearest sidewalk toll booth and takes his place in the line waiting there. He is sweating profusely, peeved at lugging his suitcase, angry at the Mayor, the city, and other New Yorkers. Standing in line waiting to pay their sidewalk tolls, the other New Yorkers joke, talk about movies and night clubs, clothes and food. Rizzoli is pissed at all these New Yorkers. *Poor*

*bastards will just roll over and play dead for anyone. ANY-
ONE! If they get their one little chance in the beginning to
gripe . . . then, whatever: Higher subway tolls, garbage
strikes, whatever! They'll take it. But TOLL SIDEWALKS?
Look at these poor devils. They pay; they always pay!*
Rizzoli wonders what happened to the great mythic
New Yorkers of old—people who didn't take any of this
shit.

"Didn't the sidewalks used to be free?" Rizzoli asks as
he moves to the head of the line, facing the toll clerk.
There's no response on the part of the surly woman inside who motions with her finger to put the money under the window.

"75th. How do I get there?" Rizzoli asks, sensing his
question has caused the others behind him to get
impatient.

"You pay a toll to go one block over 72nd to Columbus," the woman tells him in a tired monotone. "Then
you pay another toll to go the three blocks up Columbus
to 75th, and another toll to go over 75th."

"WHAT? NO WAY!" Rizzoli hollers. "There must be
some way to get four blocks to 75th without all this
rigmarole."

"COME ON, BUDDY! WE HAVEN'T GOT ALL DAY," someone
hollers from the back of the line.

"Can somebody just explain these sidewalks?" Rizzoli
asks in utter frustration, "I'm confused."

"Here, let me explain it to you," some sweet old lady
says, stepping out of line and taking Rizzoli to the side.
She, too, mistakes him for a tourist as she explains that
the toll sidewalk system here in New York City is simple, really.

SIMPLE? Rizzoli is embarrassed that a little old lady has to explain the city to him. He tells her he wants to go to 75th, between Columbus and the Park.

"In order to get to 75th between Columbus and the Park," she explains patiently, "you first have the Metropolitan Life Insurance toll, that covers 72nd from the Hudson River to Central Park. Then you have the Blue Cross-Blue Shield Health Insurance toll on Columbus from Lincoln Center up to 86th and, on 75th, you have the Trump toll."

Trump? He bought the sidewalks on my street? Rizzoli wonders. *What's happened to my neighborhood?* He's suddenly saddened at how much the Upper West Side has changed. *Fancy shoe stores and gourmet ice cream were one thing but CORPORATELY OWNED PAY SIDEWALKS?*

The old lady explains where Rizzoli pays his tolls and that the cost would be $5.80: $2 to Columbus; $3 up Columbus; and 80¢ for the half block on 75th.

$5.80? Rizzoli is in a daze. He asks, "Is there any way I can get there and not pay so much in tolls?"

"Certainly," she says with a smile, "you can take the overhead MTS.

"MTS?" Rizzoli asks.

"Municipal Thruway Sidewalk, I'm sorry. We call it the MTS."

WE? Rizzoli is stunned to hear himself suddenly excluded, as he's always been proud to be included in "We New Yorkers."

"Overhead, there," she points in back of Rizzoli to Broadway. "It's faster and cheaper than street level."

Rizzoli turns to see a Broadway he has never seen before, one he somehow missed first getting out of the subway stop. *I didn't look up. I guess I was so busy looking at the crowded sidewalks down here . . . shit, what the hell is it?* Overhead, suspended five stories up, running as far as the eye can see in both directions on Broadway, Rizzoli sees an elevated walkway suspended between buildings on either side of the street with no undergirding.

"It's run by the city," the old lady continues, "and you pay one set toll to get on. With that you can walk whatever distance you want without having to pay another toll."

Rizzoli senses Mayor Jimmy the Whack's hand behind all of this as he asks how much the city thruway toll is.

"A dollar fifty," she says, "so you save more than four dollars, and it's not crowded."

Where Broadway swerves left going uptown, Rizzoli can see that up on the thruway, people are walking along very fast. *And there's no crowd*, Rizzoli observes, with great relief.

"It's a deal," she says.

"It *is* a deal," Rizzoli answers before he realizes this is what the Mayor wants him to think. *A DEAL? WHAT AM I DOING? I'M PLAYING RIGHT INTO JIMMY THE WHACK'S HANDS.* He looks at the crowds again. *But, Jimmy has left me no choice.*

The crowds on the hot sidewalks compel Rizzoli to ask the old lady one question. "With it so uncrowded up there, why would anyone be down here on one of these sidewalks?"

"Simple," she says. "New Yorkers have to get groceries and dry cleaning and the stores are down here."

The answer should have been obvious to him all along,

Rizzoli thinks. He tells her he thinks he'll take the Thruway.

She tells him to take the Broadway Thruway up to 81st, then get the crosstown Thruway over 81st and the Central Park West Thruway down to 75th—all for $1.50. "It's a deal," she repeats. Then, she tells Rizzoli that to get on the Broadway Thruway you take the elevator up to the fifth floor in that apartment building, walk to the end of the hallway, pay a toll at the booth, and go out onto the Thruway.

Rizzoli thanks her and follows her instructions. At the toll booth on the fifth floor, he stands with his suitcase in a small line waiting to pay. Outside on the Thruway, he sees pedestrians and joggers streaming by at a fast, steady pace. Rizzoli pays and joins the stream of people going uptown on the Thruway

People zoom by him as Rizzoli starts off at a slower pace, in the middle lane, lugging his suitcase and sweating big circles onto his shirt. *You know it's like the New York State Thruway for cars, . . . only it's people*, Rizzoli thinks as he glances up at the big green signs with white lettering overhead. Everyone going by Rizzoli is walking as fast as he possibly can. *Some serious walkers here*, Rizzoli thinks as he tries to pick up his pace and keep up. His suitcase keeps holding him back, however, and more and more walkers zoom by.

"TWWEEEEEEEEET" A whistle blows behind Rizzoli. He turns around and sees a jogger slowed to almost running in place who is signaling for Rizzoli to move to the slower outside lane. Rizzoli refuses: the jogger keeps right on after him. *This ding-a-ling is tailgating me or something*, Rizzoli thinks before moving to the side. The jogger zips by and disappears up ahead. Rizzoli puts his head down and races along with the others as fast as he can, with sweat flying off him.

When Rizzoli finally lifts his head up, he reads on the big, green overhead sign: "EXIT 13. 86TH ST. NEXT RIGHT." He's passed 81st Street, EXIT 12, the one the lady told him about. *And now I have to go to 86th . . . ten blocks more out of my way . . . in this heat . . . for Jimmy the Whack. What am I, LOONIE TUNES?*

Rizzoli continues along in the slow lane reading all the signs methodically now so he doesn't miss the 86th Street Turnoff. He reads:

"USE FLASHERS UNDER 4 MPH"

Flashers?

"YIELD"

"EMERGENCY STOPPING ONLY"

"REDUCED SPEED AHEAD."

At Exit 13 Rizzoli gets off and goes through the turnstile out into the hallway of an apartment where he takes the elevator down to street level once again. *But, I'm not going back by Thruway—I'll drop dead from the heat.*

Rizzoli waits in line to pay the Chemical Bank toll, the first of five tolls he'll have to pay to get to 75th by street-level sidewalks. While waiting, Rizzoli puts on his Walkman to try and get some soothing music. He turns it on and hears Jimmy the Whack saying:

" . . . the idea was mine from the beginning. To keep corporations from leaving Manhattan and going to Jersey to get lower taxes, I had to do something new and drastic. In the past I'd tried every incentive possible to keep the corporations here—energy subsidies, tax breaks—then I hit on toll sidewalks."

Jimmy the Whack is relentless. Rizzoli thinks, exhausted. For the first time ever, the Mayor's words are like sledgehammer blows to Rizzoli's spirit.

"I thought, 'Let New York City's corporations buy blocks of sidewalks and charge pedestrians passing by. Jersey can't match that—for one, they don't have the millions of pedestrians all wedged into such a small piece of real estate as we do in Manhattan."

YOU HALF WIT! Rizzoli mutters. *Try, try, but, you're never going to break my spirit.*

". . . so, I say, 'Fine, the corporations get a new source of profit, but what's in it for the city?' That's when I think of the elevated pedestrian Thruway run by City Hall. New Yorkers are going to want to escape the crowded, penned-in, street-level corporate sidewalks, right, am I right?"

"*SHUT UP!*" Rizzoli screams out loud. No one else in line pays any attention to Rizzoli: they just assume he is another street crazy as he continues hollering, "SHUT UP, YOU HALF-WIT!" while listening to the Mayor continue:

". . . so, like the city advertises, people have to come up to the city way of walking."

"First we incited the mass hostility that welled up when there were toll sidewalks and nothing else," O'Dilly says, "then we channeled this hostility constructively into the overhead Thruway, and New Yorkers were glad we could do something to relieve their intense frustration."

The Mayor agrees with O'Dilly and then addresses himself to the host's last question: "What is the future of the toll sidewalk system?"

"Possibly, we'll sell off the present fifth floor Thruway in segments to different corporations. They can charge separate tolls like they do now on the street level. Then, after hostility has built up over that, the city will go higher still to the ninth floor, say, and build a new second Thruway there and then sell that off to the corporations. Then build another third Thruway higher up still, and so on and on, so New Yorkers will always have to come up to a higher level to escape the corporations and contribute revenue to our great, great city."

"First, you incite mass hostility," says the Commissioner of Hostility, "then you channel it in a constructive way."

"If the corporations are happy, the city is happy, and the pedestrians will fall in line," the mayor concludes.

Not me, Rizzoli vows. *I'll never fall in line.* He pays his toll like all the others and moves along 86th, carrying his suitcase and wondering if he even has a job or an apartment—*after his time away. However long that was.*

He sees a pay phone, calls his office and asks for his boss, Mr. Whittaker.

"Mr. Witty-tak-i? No Witty-tak-i here."

Rizzoli hangs up. He calls Louie at the newsstand. When an unfamiliar voice answers, Rizzoli asks, "Louie Stella? Mr. Louie Stella?"

"Stelli? Stelli? WOO-IE *WHO?*"

Rizzoli hangs up. *It's New York—what can you do? Nobody ever said living here was easy. You gotta love it—see the humorous side. It's not gonna get me down. What's a job and the old neighborhood? When you got to battle this bonkers toll system . . . or give in to Jimmy the Whack.*

Rizzoli finally sees a newsstand. He buys a *Times* and checks the date. It's only been three weeks since he's been gone. *What can I expect? Here, they throw up a skyscraper overnight. It's the city that never sleeps. Changes occur . . . things happen . . . the city rolls on . . . if you stay away, you gotta expect changes.*

A DREAM OF RIZZOLI Off and on for days Rizzoli
IN LOVE IN THE has hailed cabs and each time be-
CAB SHARING WAY fore getting in he goes through
the same split second ritual. With the cab door open,
Rizzoli gives his destination. Then he waits precious seconds in the hope that, somehow, she will appear unex-
pectedly at his side and say, "Maybe we can share a cab.
I'm going that way, too." He closes his eyes, hoping he
will hear her say these words. Silence. He hesitates another split-second before twirling around, expecting to
see her at his side, as if by magic. Nothing.

*Every time before it's been like this, too. Will she ever
appear?* Rizzoli wonders. *Why do I keep thinking I'll see
her for the first time ever?*

"You in or out?" the cabbie asks.

Rizzoli says, "In. In. I'm in."

Rizzoli gets in. The cab starts off. As he glides through
Manhattan, Rizzoli continues to think about her, as he
has for days now. *I dream of her, I see her,* he wonders,
but, will she ever appear?

She might never appear, a strange voice suddenly says
amidst Rizzoli's thoughts. It startles him. *Even so,* the
voice continues, *you can call her "Phoenicia."*

Phoenicia. The name is exactly right, Rizzoli thinks, and
like magic, its sound makes him suddenly see her more
clearly than ever before. Now, in his mind, her image
floats before him. *She wears red shoes and a short summer
dress. Her cropped black hair frames her small, heart-
shaped face.* Rizzoli is excited by the way her shapely legs
taper down into her red high heels. *THE RED SHOES!* It's
almost too much for Rizzoli—he tells himself: *She has to
appear. Phoenicia HAS to appear.*

No. Phoenicia doesn't HAVE *to appear,* the strange voice interrupts. *You knew that when you got into cab sharing. You chose cab sharing. It's the one way you wanted to risk falling in love.*

CAB SHARING? *That* VOICE? Rizzoli thinks, *Am I crazy? To have that* VOICE *talking to me? I didn't choose . . . what is it? . . . when did I choose it?*

Don't play dumb, Rizzoli, That Voice says, *you elected cab sharing—trying to fall in love with Phoenicia that way excites you—so, you chose it.*

I did? Rizzoli is dumbfounded.

You did. You did, That Voice says. *You now have to trust that somewhere in this huge city sometime next to some cab you just hailed, Phoenicia will appear for the first time and ask you to share a cab. Of course, you risk that she'll never appear.*

Never?

Never, That Voice repeats. *You understood that risk when you elected Cab Sharing.* LOVE IS RISK. YOU'RE RISK-ING LOVE, RIZZOLI

Maybe this explains why I'm not myself lately, Rizzoli thinks. *But this confuses me more. Phoenicia? I want to know how this all came about.*

How? That Voice asks incredulously. HOW? *"How" has no meaning in Cab Sharing Love.* IF *you're falling in love this way, Rizzoli, "how" becomes a nonsense word. There is no "how," only "if."*

That Voice stuns Rizzoli into a hazy realization: *What must I have done to choose this Cab Sharing mess?* Even though he can't remember when or how he chose it, Rizzoli thinks, *I chose it, according to That Voice, that's all that matters now—I'm in it. What can I do? I* MUST BE AN

IDIOT! Why else would I blindly go along in the first place, searching for a certain unknown woman to share a cab with me—A TOTAL STRANGER—in a city of seven million? I'M AN IDIOT!

You didn't have to choose to torture yourself like this, that Voice tells Rizzoli. *You could have chosen to remain friends with women on the OUTSIDE of cabs only, and never RISKED getting into cab sharing with one certain woman.*

I could have? Rizzoli wonders.

Of course, That Voice answers, *there are more convenient, easier ways of being in love—Over-the-Road Trucking, for one. There you have set dates to meet . . . no torturing yourself about IF she will show up. She shows up, pure and simple, time and time again so over long periods of being together, the love slowly builds. Like a shrub growing, not KAPOW like in Cab Sharing.*

TRUCKING? So why didn't I choose trucking? Rizzoli asks the Voice. *Who needs all this mishegoss? Why?*

WHY? That Voice answers Rizzoli. *Because you believe Cab Sharing is the only REAL WAY to be in love—it's got it all—excitement, daring, mystery, uncertainty, the passion of finally coming together with Phoenicia—or not. Falling in love—or not. Staying in love—or not.*

Wait! Rizzoli interjects as the cab stops at his destination. *How do I know this Phoenicia I'm waiting for even exists? I've never seen her, I only imagined that was her name moments ago. I see her face, I feel her body, but only in my imagination. Maybe she doesn't exist?*

Maybe not, That Voice says.

What? Rizzoli answers, *Don't say that.*

"Hey, buddy, shit or get off the pot," the cabbie suddenly says. "You payin' or what?"

"Sure. Sure," Rizzoli says. "I'm paying, I'm paying."

In the next few days Rizzoli takes many cabs, sometimes two, three in an hour, often unnecessarily. He can't help himself. *It's expensive, sure,* he thinks, *but it's worth it.* By doing this constantly he reminds himself the chances of her suddenly appearing at his side to share a cab are greatly increased.

This day Rizzoli pays the fare for one cab then moves twenty feet to the cross street and hails another cab to take him right back to where the first cab picked him up on Columbus Avenue. *No Phoenicia, if there IS a Phoenicia,* Rizzoli thinks as he gets in this cab.

The cab speeds him right back to where he started with the last cab. Rizzoli thinks, *If only I had clarified this Cab Sharing type of love beforehand, I might have been able to meet Phoenicia at a set time and place to share a fare.*

NO WAY, says That Voice. *Any prearrangement breaks the cardinal rule of Cab Sharing Love. That rule is: YOU CAN NEVER PIN ANYTHING DOWN OR YOU RUIN IT.*

Cab Sharing Love. The thought of it unnerves Rizzoli now as the cab brings him to the curb on Columbus Avenue. He pays the fare, gets out, and, as he starts for home, he vows to get a hold of himself.

The next week Rizzoli is composed. He has finally ceased pining so much for her. He hails cabs with only a slight ache that she will still appear. He feels that ache now as he sees three yellow cabs with riders go by, then watches as a blue gypsy cab pulls over to the curb at 57th and Madison.

"Fifth and 34th," Rizzoli says to the cabbie when he hears a soft female voice say, "Would you like to share a cab? I'm going to Lord and Taylor on Fifth."

Rizzoli turns around and sees a very appealing woman in a black suit and black high heels with auburn hair pulled back in a bun and a soft, expressive face with a warm smile. *But it's probably not Phoenicia*, Rizzoli concludes before smiling back and saying, "Fine. Sure."

Who is this? Rizzoli wonders as they get in the cab.

You don't know. She's a mystery, That Voice informs Rizzoli. *A total mystery at this point.*

Rizzoli and the woman start to talk and almost instantly he thinks, *It's as if we've talked before.* With the cab now backed up on 57th heading for Fifth Avenue, they have begun talking about restaurants. Fifth Avenue is jammed, and with their cab stalled again they talk about a recent movie they've both seen.

They approach Lord and Taylor, and by now Rizzoli is sure he knows her name even before he asks her.

"Phoenicia," she says. "And yours?"

"Rizzoli."

"Rizzoli. I like that name. Maybe we'll meet again," she says, as the cab pulls to the curb.

As she smiles and passes over her share of the fare, Rizzoli is about to ask her her last name so he can arrange to see her again soon.

NO, NO. That Voice butts in, *even now that you met her you cannot arrange a set time to see her again. You have to TRUST she'll show up again.*

Even now after I've met her I have to go through this?

She gathers her purse and reaches for the door. Rizzoli gets frantic. *Make arrangements or you'll never see her again, you dimwit—never—ever!*

NO. That Voice counters, *Do that and you BLOW IT.*

Now as Phoenicia stands on the sidewalk smiling and waving, the debate in Rizzoli's mind turns raucous. *DO IT,* Rizzoli urges himself. *DON'T DO IT,* That Voice says.

PIN IT DOWN, AND YOU SCREW UP EVERYTHING, That Voice warns Rizzoli. *PIN IT DOWN,* RIZZOLI, Rizzoli urges himself.

Screw That Voice, Rizzoli finally tells himself. Holding the cab door open, he leans out to try and set up a future date with her. "Phoenicia?

Do it then, That Voice says, *but, don't blame me when you never see her again. DO IT.*

Rizzoli pauses.

"Yes?" Phoenicia says, turning around smiling.

Trust you'll see her again, Rizzoli, that's all you can do in cab sharing love: TRUST.

Shut up, Rizzoli tells That Voice, smiling all the while at Phoenicia. In the end, Rizzoli says very sweetly, but casually, "Maybe we *will* meet again. That would be nice."

"It would," Phoenicia says, as the cab edges away. She waves; Rizzoli waves back through the cab's rear window. As she walks away up the street, Rizzoli stares, noticing how her shapely calves taper into her black high heels. He imagines her in red high heels and thinks, *Oh, Phoenicia . . . Phoenicia.*

Then reality comes home to Rizzoli. *I don't even know her last name or where she works and now she's disappeared. I should have found out those details.*

You can NEVER ask those details, That Voice says. *Knowing those particular things about her—where she works, her*

address, phone number— would be against the rules of Cab Sharing love. Same for her. She can never know these particulars about you.

WHAT? Rizzoli is outraged. *You mean I could never call her for a date ever? Even if I wanted to? Because I'll NEVER know her last name?* Phoenicia has long disappeared . . . but Rizzoli still stares out the rear window after her. *Why'd I ever do this?* he wonders. *Will she show up again?*

That's it, says That Voice. *You don't say, "She will show up. Or she'll never show up. You ask yourself, "Will she show up?" and then she just might. Never get clutchy, for Cab Sharing, keep loose—keep loose.*

Rizzoli doesn't take well to That Voice's coaching, but he listens in spite of himself:

In Cab Sharing Love, the ride itself is everything. What goes on inside the cab is everything. You can't will it. When the time comes, you ride . . . you can't make it happen. When the right cab comes, and she's suddenly there again, you just ride.

"What was your destination, again?" the cab driver is asking.

———

Over the next few days, Rizzoli practices staying loose by repeating to himself various prescriptive sayings that he suspects originated with That Voice, but he can't be sure of this since That Voice has not spoken directly to him since that day in the cab with Phoenicia. Nonetheless, Rizzoli keeps telling himself from time to time:

Nothing I can do will make Phoenicia reappear. She has to show up of her own free will.

I can accept that Phoenicia might not show up again ever,
but at least I saw her that once.
I have a choice in this, too. I could refuse to hail cabs but
I don't choose to do that. I choose to hail cabs and give
her the chance, somewhere, sometime, to share another
cab.

A week later at Sheridan Square in the Village, Rizzoli
hails a cab. Phoenicia appears out of nowhere. They
laugh at their chance second meeting. They go uptown.
They talk about some current Broadway shows, and she
mentions her grandmother once worked at Minsky's.
Rizzoli accepts it all as a mystery. He tells her his father
once heard Enrico Caruso sing live at the old Met.

For the next week he stays loose, and the looseness
brings surprises. Two days later, at Broadway and
110th, he runs into Phoenicia a third time, and they
share a cab downtown. It's a Saturday and she's dressed
casually, in shorts, with her hair down around her
shoulders. Rizzoli is enthralled. They talk about being
single in the city. She is touched by something he says
and brushes his cheek with her hand.

Then he sees her a fourth and a fifth time. They are
getting very relaxed with one another now. The next
chance meeting they ride together laughing at a very
funny street scene they see in front of Tiffany's: a man,
naked from the waist up, with a Bowler Hat walking an
iguana on a leash. They kiss before she has to get out for
what she says is "a very important appointment."

Rizzoli doesn't ask for specifics: now he forgets to
think of the particulars. She doesn't ask him either. It's
futile to ask, Rizzoli knows. *And not really necessary to*

know. Funny, now it's becoming second nature for us not to ask. Without the particulars, I will surely see her again, no, might, he thinks, MIGHT *see her again.*

————

Rizzoli does see her again, but this time they fight before he has to get off at his stop. The fight starts over some little thing, the best direction to give the cabbie. Before completing the short ride to Rizzoli's destination, they're shouting at one another. He doesn't want to, but he has to get out. As he leaves, she slams the cab door shut on him.

Then, when the cab is gone and Rizzoli is standing on the street corner staring after it, That Voice suddenly returns: *Inside the cab is the whole ball game. There, any instant, she could blow it—you could blow it.*

What is this? I don't need to hear this, Rizzoli tells That Voice. *SHUT UP!*

That Voice goes on: *Then again you two could make it and, actually fall in love. Nobody knows how it will turn out in Cab Sharing. But, one thing is certain, whatever happens between you two inside the cab is the whole megillah.*

SHUT UP, Rizzoli tells That Voice. then thinks that he should try to find her by tracing her life from some of her previous stops.

That's futile, That Voice says. *Outside the cab, she has her own life that you can never know. You can only wonder. When you are separated, you can never know what she will do. You can only TRUST you'll come together with her again INSIDE the cab.*

Inside the cab is the whole megillah, Rizzoli suddenly

realizes, with full impact. *My God!*

———

Rizzoli spends the days afterward hailing hundreds of cabs. Phoenicia is never there. *I know it*, he thinks, *I'll never see her again.* He blames himself. *I did it. Fighting like that left a bad impression.*

Love is never forever, you know that, Rizzoli.

It's That Voice again. Rizzoli thinks.

Maybe she got hit by a bus That Voice says, *or, she might be sharing a cab with someone else this very instant. Maybe she changed to being in love with someone else in over-the-road trucking style. It's her choice.*

PHOENICIA? OVER-THE-ROAD TRUCKING? SHE CHOSE A TEAMSTER LOVER OVER ME? Rizzoli is crestfallen.

Maybe she did, That Voice answers. *You don't know. All you can do is* TRUST. *Be accepting and she might show up again.*

Rizzoli dislikes having to credit That Voice, but afterwards he does admit to himself, *I have to stay loose. I'm clutching.*

Rizzoli works on it until he finally accepts she might be gone forever. He takes fewer cabs, yet he still hopes to run into her. He doesn't.

Now as he hails a cab in front of the Chrysler Building, the last thing he expects to hear is a female voice saying, "Would you like to share a cab, Rizzoli?" He barely believes he heard it. He turns around. It's her. "Phoenicia! I've missed you."

Phoenicia is radiant, her face warm and expressive. "I've missed you, too." She hugs him. "I even worried you might have stopped taking cabs," she says. "I hoped you wouldn't do that."

Rizzoli smiles and kisses her. They get in the cab. They quickly decide their argument occurred over a trifle so ridiculous as to be wildly funny. They giggle. They laugh. They talk. They tell the cabbie to turn off the meter. In between bursts of talk they hug and kiss as the cab slowly weaves and wanders through Manhattan.

It has been two months since they've seen one another, so they talk hurriedly to catch up. At one point, Phoenicia breathlessly tells him about being terrified to do something at work and then deciding to do it anyway by putting on an act of self-assurance. "It was just an act," she says, "but I got through it, and my boss said afterward, 'These things never seem to faze you, Phoenicia. I'm amazed. I would be terrified.' " She and Rizzoli get the giggles.

Rizzoli tells her one about a recent episode in which his own genuine gratitude was mistaken for vanity, when his "Thank you" sounded like "a bank full." She laughs more. They hug and laugh together.

Rizzoli marvels that their long conversation has again been devoid of any particulars about either of their lives. They both do this effortlessly now.

It's beginning to work . . . this cab sharing.

Phoenicia checks her watch and remembers she has to be somewhere in a half hour. She has the cab leave her at Washington Square.

Phoenicia gets out and blows Rizzoli a kiss.

Rizzoli blows her a kiss back.

The cab pulls off, and Rizzoli wonders: *Outside the cab, what is she like?* He knows he can never know.

When I'm outside the cab, she must wonder, what is Rizzoli like? He smiles to himself and muses about the mystery of it all.

"Your stop, sir," the cabbie says.

———

Over the next month, Rizzoli keeps real loose but it doesn't seem to help because Phoenicia still doesn't show up. He accepts this. Secretly, though, he suspects that she is the one who now has become clutchy, not him.

Rizzoli stays loose for another week, but when Phoenicia still doesn't show up, he gives in to agony. *I knew it,* he thinks. *She's never going to be able to get a hold of herself. I'll never see her again after that last time. I knew I was never going to see her again.*

Rizzoli panics; he hails fourteen cabs in one day.

Nothing.

Then he remembers and tells himself: *I think I'll see her again but I can never know that for sure. I trust she is thinking the same. We both have to be, to come together; it's the basis of cab sharing love. I chose it. I can accept it either way.*

Now calm, accepting, Rizzoli hails his fifteenth and last cab for the day when he hears a voice say, "Do you want to share a cab, Rizzoli?"

Rizzoli turns and sees Phoenicia looking relieved. Now he understands what it takes for both of them to come together in one of these chance encounters. He hugs her. They kiss more passionately than ever before.

"So what's it goin' to be?" the cabbie says, as they stay

lost in their kiss. "Yo?"

They laugh and get in the cab, and Rizzoli notices Phoenicia is wearing red high heels. *THE RED SHOES! Rizzoli thinks, suddenly inflamed at the sight of her tanned legs narrowing down into . . . the red shoes.*

Phoenicia smiles. Rizzoli tells the cabbie to turn off the meter and just drive. The cab weaves past the Empire State Building, Grand Central, the United Nations. The East River glides by, with boats passing in the gathering dusk. She moans; Rizzoli soars. Phoenicia's red high heels stand upright on the cab's floor. *The red shoes . . . like twins,* Rizzoli thinks.

After making love, they whisper sweetly as the cab slides through the twilight that now turns the Chrysler Building into brilliant roses and golds. He holds her in his arms and they talk until the windows of the skyscrapers are checkered with lights against the night.

Hours later, the cabbie asks, "How much you wanna spend?" and announces their total. The fare takes nearly all the money they both have together, so they arrange to have the cabbie let them off soon at separate stops. Although neither wants to leave the cab, they know they'll have to.

Rizzoli's stop is first. By the time it nears, he has his suit and rumpled white shirt on again, with his tie hanging loose. Phoenicia smooths out his sports jacket. She, too, is dressed again and looking the way she did when she first got in the cab, only with a strand of her hair loose. They embrace and kiss.

"Yo, my man . . . ," says the cabbie, eager to get going.

It's the last thing Rizzoli wants to do but he knows

there's no other way. He gives her his share of the fare, kisses her one last time and exits.

The cab pulls away. Rizzoli waves as Phoenicia stares back at him out the rear window. Then she disappears into the night.

Rizzoli shivers as he stands alone on the deserted street. It is a cold night. He remembers that he forgot his trenchcoat in the cab. It makes no difference.

———————

They continue sharing many cabs together. But neither will say for certain it will happen again until it does happen. Then, next to some cab, sometime, somewhere, in this great city, they embrace.

Now, this latest time, inside the cab, as Phoenicia talks, Rizzoli's mind drifts off. Even as he watches her talking, he hears her voice fade. He observes with surprise that she has streaks of gray in her hair. He can't hear her voice any longer. *What do I care about Phoenicia's gray hair,* Rizzoli muses. *It has nothing to do with what goes on here in the cab.* He vows, *I'll always love her no matter how she ages. Who cares?*

She becomes fully gray now as Rizzoli gazes upon her. It's Phoenicia's stop but he notes, *She seems eager not to have to leave the cab, now that she has aged.*

As the cab turns the next corner, Rizzoli glances out the window at a three-card monte game and, in that moment, for the first time, he sees his own image reflected. He is white-haired with deep creases in his cheeks and liver spots. *My God, how long has it been we've been sharing cabs? Fifty years? I must be the Rip Van*

Rizzoli of Cab Sharing.

Phoenicia must have noticed, Rizzoli thinks, *but she didn't say anything.* He asks Phoenicia and she tells him; of course she noticed. "But why mention it," she says, "if it was not important?"

Rizzoli agrees; he is very touched they've been together this long . . . *in love in the cab sharing way.*

At her stop, Phoenicia gets out of the cab and waves. Rizzoli wishes more than ever before that she could stay here in the cab with him. *Why can't we just stay in the cab together forever?* He wonders, as the cab drives on without her.

Alone in the back, Rizzoli senses something is wrong this time. Underneath his feet, the cab's drive shaft starts making clunking sounds and the cabbie explains that tonight is his Checker cab's last run forever. The cabbie says, "Ya know, all dis freakin' time, I really thought I'd croak before her. No way. Ya never know about dem t'ings, right?"

"Right," Rizzoli says.

"Rizzoli, what is it?" Phoenicia asks. "Are you dreaming? You must have dozed off."

Rizzoli awakes and sees it's Phoenicia and she has her red shoes on her hands walking them up his stomach. She is young and pretty; her face as warm and expressive as ever. "Phoenicia. Phoenicia." Rizzoli draws her to him.

Love is never forever, That Voice suddenly says. *Nothing is forever. Who knows, Rizzoli, come tomorrow, you might want to look into over-the-road trucking with a different woman?*

I might. Rizzoli answers. He's learned how to play

That Voice by now. *You never know.* He knows over-the-road would never be for him.

Now, as the city passes by, the lovers embrace in the back of the cab, their eyes closed, oblivious to the buildings being torn down and the new ones going up.

"Be a great city, if dey ever finish it," the cabbie says to no one in particular. "Ain't dat what dey always say?"

Silence.

RIZZOLI RUNS Rizzoli dreams that he is running through the streets of Manhattan in a group of ten, all of them wearing T-shirts saying, "New Yorkers Are Real People."

Soon one has to leave to begin a novel about his wife.

Now there are nine "New Yorkers Are Real People" running in the streets.

A man is struck by a workman's thermos falling from the seventy-sixth floor of an unfinished office tower.

Now there are eight "New Yorkers Are Real People" running in the streets.

A man thinks he must have cancer or kidney failure and leaves to see a doctor.

Now there are seven "New Yorkers Are Real People" running in the streets.

One has to leave to see her analyst.

Now there are six "New Yorkers Are Real People" running in the streets.

One talks nonstop about his job and nothing else, until the others say "Go away."

Now there are five "New Yorkers Are Real People" running in the streets.

One runs faster and faster and faster until no one can keep up. He has a bad heart to begin with, and the others are worried but can't do anything to stop him.

Now there are four "New Yorkers Are Real People" running in the streets.

One looks in a shop window, sees her own image reflected, and can't tear herself away from it.

Now there are three "New Yorkers Are Real People" running in the streets.

One keeps worrying about whether or not he turned

off the gas burner on the stove in his apartment. Finally, he has to leave and run sixty-seven blocks home to see.

Now Rizzoli and his friend Cheswick are the last two "New Yorkers Are Real People" running in the streets.

Cheswick says to Rizzoli, "There are some things I've always wanted to say to you but I never felt I could mention them."

"What? Feel free," Rizzoli says to his old friend.

"One thing I've never been able to stand about you, Rizzoli," Cheswick says, "is the way you slurp your coffee."

"Why didn't you say something?"

"I never wanted to hurt your feelings. What's more," Cheswick goes on, "when you get excited I can't stand the tone of your voice. It drives me *nuts*," he says. "Nuts. And why wave your hands when you're excited? That's a bit much, Rizzoli, don't you think?"

Before Rizzoli can answer, Cheswick stops and walks away in a huff.

Now Rizzoli is the last of the "New Yorkers Are Real People" running in the streets.

He's running as fast as he can.

Obelisk Paperbacks

GILBERT ADAIR
Alice Through the Needle's Eye
DONALD BARTHELME
Sixty Stories
ADOLFO BIOY CASARES
Asleep in the Sun
Diary of the War of the Pig
The Dream of Heroes
JANE BOWLES
Two Serious Ladies
ANITA BROOKNER
Hotel du Lac
Look at Me
Providence
LEONORA CARRINGTON
The House of Fear
The Seventh Horse
MARK CIABATTARI
Dreams of an Imaginary New Yorker Named Rizzoli
NOËL COWARD
Pomp and Circumstance
Star Quality: The Collected Stories of Noël Coward
PETER FARB
Man's Rise to Civilization
LAWRENCE FERLINGHETTI
Love in the Days of Rage
PATRICK GALE
The Aerodynamics of Pork
Ease
Kansas in August
JOHN GARDNER
The Wreckage of Agathon
NELSON GEORGE
The Death of Rhythm & Blues
MOLLY KEANE
Good Behaviour
Time After Time
WILLIAM KOTZWINKLE
The Exile
The Fan Man
ERIC KRAFT
Herb 'n' Lorna
JAMES McCONKEY
Court of Memory
COLIN MacINNES
Absolute Beginners
GREIL MARCUS
Mystery Train

COVER ART BY ISTVAN BANYAI
COVER DESIGN BY DIANE GOLDSMITH
AUTHOR PHOTO BY JANE CIABATTARI